Now that the weath[...]
the sun with this mo[...]
reads from Harlequi[...]

Favorite author Lucy Monroe brings you
Bought: The Greek's Bride, the first installment
in her MEDITERRANEAN BRIDES duet. Two
billionaires are out to claim their brides—but
have they met their match? Read Sandor's story now
and Miguel's next month! Meanwhile, Miranda Lee's
The Ruthless Marriage Proposal is the sensuous
tale of a housekeeper who falls in love with her
handsome billionaire boss.

If it's a sexy sheikh you're after,
The Sultan's Virgin Bride by Sarah Morgan
has a ruthless sultan determined to have
the one woman he can't. In Kim Lawrence's
The Italian's Wedding Ultimatum an Italian's
seduction leads to passion and pregnancy!
The international theme continues with
Kept by the Spanish Billionaire by Cathy Williams,
where playboy Rafael Vives is shocked when his
mistress of the moment turns out to be much more.

In Robyn Donald's *The Blackmail Bargain*
Curt blackmails Peta, unaware that she's a penniless
virgin. And Lee Wilkinson's *Wife by Approval* is
the story of a handsome wealthy heir who needs
glamorous Valentina to secure his birthright.

Finally, there's Natalie Rivers with her debut novel,
The Kristallis Baby, where an arrogant Greek tycoon
claims his orphaned nephew—by taking virginal
Carrie's innocence and wedding her. Happy reading!

GREEK TYCOONS

They're the men who have everything—
except brides...

Wealth, power, charm—
what else could a heart-stoppingly handsome
tycoon need? In the GREEK TYCOONS
miniseries you have already been introduced
to some gorgeous Greek multimillionaires
that are in need of wives.

Now it's the turn of brand-new
Harlequin Presents author Natalie Rivers,
with her thrilling romance,
The Kristallis Baby

This tycoon has met his match, and he's decided
he *has* to have her...*whatever* that takes!

Natalie Rivers

THE KRISTALLIS BABY

GREEK
TYCOONS

HARLEQUIN®

TORONTO • NEW YORK • LONDON
AMSTERDAM • PARIS • SYDNEY • HAMBURG
STOCKHOLM • ATHENS • TOKYO • MILAN • MADRID
PRAGUE • WARSAW • BUDAPEST • AUCKLAND

ISBN-13: 978-0-373-12642-2
ISBN-10: 0-373-12642-5

THE KRISTALLIS BABY

First North American Publication 2007.

www.eHarlequin.com

Printed in U.S.A.

All about the author...
Natalie Rivers

NATALIE RIVERS grew up in the Sussex countryside. As a child she always loved to lose herself in a good book or in games that gave free rein to her imagination. She went to Sheffield University, where she met her husband in the first week of term. It was love at first sight and they have been together ever since. They moved to London after graduating, got married and had two wonderful children.

After university Natalie worked in a lab at a medical research charity and later retrained to be a primary school teacher. She began writing when her son started nursery school, giving her a couple of free mornings a week. Now she is lucky enough to be able to combine her two favorite occupations—being a full-time mom and writing passionate romances. When she has a free moment, she enjoys reading, gardening and spending time with family and friends.

For my sister, Claire.

PROLOGUE

CARRIE stared numbly at the four coffins lined up across the chapel. Apart from little baby Danny, snuggled in her arms, nothing seemed real. How could it be real? How could four people she loved be dead?

She and Danny were alone in the front pew. She shifted him on her lap so that she could look into his face, and the moment they made eye contact a massive grin lit up his features. She smiled back at him tremulously and let the priest's words wash over her. If she listened to what he was saying she knew she'd start weeping.

She couldn't let herself think about her beloved cousin Sophie and her husband Leonidas, or about the aunt and uncle who had brought her up. She couldn't think about the terrible motorway accident that had killed them all and left Danny an orphan or she knew her grief would overwhelm her. If she gave in to it now she might never stop crying. For Danny's sake she had to be strong.

He was all that she had now.

Slowly she became aware that organ music was playing, and she realised the service was over. She stood up stiffly and walked out of the chapel, holding Danny close to her chest. At twenty-five years old, the only other funeral Carrie had ever attended was her mother's, but she'd been very young at the time and had no memory of it now.

Making the arrangements for today had been a daunting prospect, and she'd had to do it all on her own. Her father hadn't helped her. He hadn't bothered to come when she'd told him about the accident, and later, when she'd called to tell him the time of the funeral, he'd almost seemed surprised.

'I can't get away at the moment,' he'd said. 'I'm completely tied up with work.'

'But it's family,' Carrie gasped. She'd learnt not to expect much from her father, but his intention to stay away from the funeral genuinely shocked her.

'Your mother's family, not mine,' he replied.

'My family, too.' She heard her voice break as she spoke. 'When you left after Mum died, they were all I had.'

'Look, it sounds like you've got everything organised,' he said, refusing to be drawn by her comments. 'You don't need me there. I'm sorry about the accident, but whether or not I come to the funeral won't make any difference to them now.'

'It would make a difference to me,' Carrie had said to the silent telephone after her father had rung off. If, just once in her life, he'd been there for her it would have meant something.

She'd wanted to tell him about her intention to care for Sophie's baby, six-month-old Danny. But how could a man who'd abandoned his own daughter as a baby understand?

She stood outside the chapel in the chill November air and clutched Danny to her. Most of the mourners had drifted away now, and the few that still lingered were talking quietly in groups. She bent her head down to press her cheek against the soft baby curls on the top of Danny's head and let out a long, shaky sigh. Soon she would be able to leave, take him away from this place of sadness.

She hadn't thought beyond the funeral. There'd been just

too much to take in. But one thing she knew for certain was that she'd always love Danny more than words could say. And she would do everything she could to make him happy.

'Miss Thomas?'

Carrie lifted her head and found herself looking at a mature man she had never seen before. He was studying her with an expression so cold and hard that it sent a shudder running through her.

'My name is Cosmo Kristallis.' His voice was deep and heavily accented.

Carrie's eyes widened in surprise. It was a shock to realise she was face to face with the estranged father of Sophie's husband, Leonidas. This man was Danny's grandfather.

'I'm so sorry about the death of your son,' she said, instinctively reaching out a hand to touch his arm.

The moment her fingers brushed the heavy woollen sleeve of his long winter overcoat she knew she'd made a mistake. Her sympathy wasn't welcome, and neither was her impudent touch.

'My son was already dead to me.' Disdain dripped from Cosmo's voice as he looked down at her hand on his sleeve. He didn't withdraw his arm or bother to shrug off her fingers. It wasn't necessary. She was already snatching her hand away, but not before she felt her fingers turn to ice.

'Then why are you here?' Carrie held her voice steady despite the unpleasant emotions that were churning through her. If he really thought so little of his own son, why had he bothered to travel from Greece to be at his funeral?

'When you contacted me to tell me about the funeral I realised there were some things I had to make plain to you,' Cosmo said. 'Specifically concerning the child you are holding.'

'Danny?' Carrie took a step backwards and wrapped her arms even tighter about the baby. What could he want with Danny?

'As I said, my son was dead to me a long time ago. I will

never acknowledge that child as a Kristallis heir,' Cosmo said, his hand gesturing towards Danny. 'That brat will never see any of my money.'

'Your money?' Carrie repeated, confused and horrified by what she was hearing. Danny was an innocent baby who had just lost both his parents. Why was this man so hostile, and why was he talking about money?

'Your cousin was a scheming little gold-digger,' Cosmo said. 'All she wanted was to get her hands on my fortune.'

'Sophie didn't want your money. All she ever wanted was to live happily with the man she loved and raise a family,' Carrie said, feeling her eyes swim with sudden tears at the thought that her cousin would never be able to live that dream now. She'd never see her child grow up.

She blinked furiously, determined not to start crying, and stared at Cosmo Kristallis coldly. Sophie and Leonidas weren't here to defend themselves, so she would have to do it. They had been good people and she'd loved them both. She wouldn't let him slander them any more.

'That child is not my grandson,' Cosmo said flatly.

'Yes, he is,' Carrie said. 'The thought that *you* are his grandfather makes me feel sick, but nevertheless he is your grandson, and I won't let you tell any more horrible lies about Sophie or Leonidas.'

'I will never acknowledge him,' Cosmo said. 'And if you ever contact my family again you will live to regret it.' Then, without giving Carrie a chance to respond, he turned and strode away.

She stared after him, realising she was shaking. She'd heard many unpleasant things about Leonidas's Greek family, but until that moment she'd never really understood why he had hated his father so much.

'It's all right. You'll never have to see that horrible man

again,' she murmured into Danny's curly brown hair. Her words were to comfort herself as much as the baby. 'We've got each other and we'll do just fine.'

CHAPTER ONE

Six months later

'PLEASE, Carrie, you've got to do this for me,' Lulu begged, streams of mascara-stained tears running down her crumpled face. 'If Darren listens to that message he'll throw me out!'

'I want to help. You know that,' Carrie said, looking at her weeping friend with concern. 'But wouldn't it be better if you did it? After all, no one's going to think twice if you walk into your husband's study and take his phone.'

'I told you—everyone heard us arguing. Anyway, I can't go down there like this,' Lulu wailed, indicating her ruined make-up with a theatrical gesture. 'But if I don't delete that message I'm going to be in such big trouble.'

'Well, *I'm* hardly going to blend in with the party.' Carrie glanced down at the sports gear she was wearing. She was Lulu's personal trainer, not one of her footballer husband's fancy party set. 'And you know I've got to leave soon or I'll be late picking up Danny.'

'It won't take long.' Lulu suddenly lunged towards her and pulled at her T-shirt. 'Quick—get these things off. You can wear one of my dresses.'

Five minutes later Carrie emerged from Lulu's bedroom,

dressed for her mission and feeling decidedly self-conscious. After the past six months of caring for Danny and coming to terms with her grief, it was an unsettling experience to dress up for a glitzy celebrity party. Even before her life had changed so dramatically she wouldn't have felt at ease in such dangerously high stiletto heels and a dress so tight she could hardly breathe. But there simply hadn't been time to sift through Lulu's wardrobe to find something she'd feel better wearing.

She left her backpack, which was stuffed rather haphazardly with her training gear, by the front door, and started moving through the house towards Darren's study. Lulu just needed his phone long enough to delete the voicemail she had left in a fit of jealousy. Then Carrie's task would be over.

She took a glass of champagne from a passing waiter and knocked back a recklessly large swallow of the sparkling liquid. An explosion of bubbles fizzed against the roof of her mouth, making her throat tighten uncomfortably and her eyes start to water. She coughed quietly, and blinked to clear her vision as she glanced quickly round the room.

Despite the early hour, the party was already in full swing. A photographer was making the rounds, finding no shortage of guests willing to pose for him—no doubt hoping to find their photos inside the glossy pages of well-known celebrity lifestyle magazines.

She smoothed the sparkly red dress over her hips in an ineffectual effort to cover a decent amount of thigh. Lulu wasn't known for choosing her wardrobe with modesty in mind, and that coupled with Carrie's considerable extra height meant that she was left with an alarming amount of leg on show. Even more disconcerting was the lack of decent coverage provided by the plunging neckline.

Feeling very self-conscious, she dropped her gaze and moved across the room. A curtain of sleek black hair fell across her eyes, but she didn't flick it back. She felt better with her face hidden—although no one was actually looking at her *face*, she thought with a shudder.

At last she slipped quietly into the study and closed the door behind her. She ignored the nerves that fluttered in her stomach and crossed to the desk. Putting her champagne glass down, she picked up Darren's jacket from the back of his chair and reached her hand into the pocket.

'Do you make a habit of that?'

Carrie gasped and spun round to see who had spoken, clutching the jacket tightly to her chest.

A stranger stood just inside the study. Tall and imposing, with an unmistakable air of power about him, he was standing perfectly still, calmly watching her every move.

Her eyes flew to his face, and as their gazes met she sucked in a startled breath. He was utterly gorgeous. Dark brown hair and bronzed skin made his appearance classically Mediterranean, apart from his eyes, which were an arresting shade of blue.

She looked at him, taking in his incredible bone structure and perfect features. He was unbelievably good-looking, but there was something disconcerting about him. She had the strangest feeling that she ought to know who he was. She bit her lip and studied him, momentarily forgetting that she was still holding the incriminating jacket.

It worried her that she couldn't place him. Many of the guests at the party were celebrities—easily recognisable people that for an instant you thought you knew, until suddenly you realised who they were. Carrie was used to that, with several of her clients being celebrities of one kind or another. But there was something about this man that unnerved her.

He was studying her in return. She felt a shiver of sexual awareness prickle across her skin as his gaze swept arrogantly over her. The intensity in his glittering blue eyes made her suddenly acutely aware of her body, and of the revealing dress she was wearing. It was an unfamiliar sensation.

For the past six months she had been totally absorbed in her new way of life. She had discovered the bittersweet joys of caring for Danny whilst dealing with the loss of so many loved ones and had learned to cope with the everyday stresses of looking after a child.

With all of that going on, she simply wasn't used to thinking of herself as an attractive woman that men might find desirable.

A wave of heat washed across her exposed skin, but it was unsettling and she did her best to ignore it. She couldn't let herself be thrown off kilter by her unexpected feelings. After all, she still had to get Darren's phone for Lulu, and then leave in time to pick up Danny.

'Can I help you?' she asked, deliberately making her voice sound as indifferent as she could. 'Are you lost, or were you looking for Darren?'

'You didn't answer *my* question,' the stranger said. 'I asked if you made a habit of that.'

Carrie's heart skipped a beat. He'd seen what she'd been up to.

'I don't know what you mean,' she said, in an attempt to brazen it out. She let the jacket fall back onto the chair, closing her fingers round the mobile phone just as her hand slid from the pocket. She tossed her silky hair away from her face and stared squarely back at him.

'I meant do you often creep into other people's studies and steal their mobile phones?' His voice was deep and resonant, with the hint of an accent that Carrie couldn't place.

'I didn't creep anywhere.' Trying to sound cool, she let her gaze slide down across his powerful body. She was impressed by what she saw. Lean and athletic, he looked amazing in his dark designer suit, but she had no doubt he'd look equally good dressed in the more revealing exercise gear that, because of her job as a trainer, she was used to seeing men wear. 'And I haven't stolen anything. This is Lulu's phone. I was fetching it for her.'

'You should really work on your story more,' he said.

'I work for Lulu.' She shrugged, trying to ignore the mocking note to his tone. Maybe she could still bluff her way out of the situation. 'She asked me to fetch it.'

'Really?' he asked, running his eyes insultingly over her, starting from the tips of her toes and working his way up in a leisurely fashion. 'Are they your work clothes?' he finished, letting his gaze linger on her almost indecently exposed breasts.

'I'm Lulu's personal trainer,' she said, trying to ignore the way her skin was burning from his perusal. It was strangely exciting, yet utterly unnerving, to feel the way her body was responding to the touch of his eyes. 'Now, please excuse me. I really must get back to her.' She took a step towards the door.

Suddenly the sound of Darren's voice right outside the study caught her attention.

Her eyes flicked nervously to the door. She still had his phone in her hand, and there was nowhere in the ridiculously skimpy outfit she was wearing to hide it. She'd made Lulu a promise, but now she wasn't going to get away with it.

She looked back at her uninvited companion. Would he give her away? Reveal that he'd caught her red-handed in the act of stealing the mobile phone?

At that moment he started walking towards her. Her heart lurched and she clutched the phone tightly, staring at him. She was paralysed like a rabbit in the glare of an approaching juggernaut. What was he going to do? Take the phone from her and tell Darren exactly what he'd seen?

His movements seemed quite unhurried, but there was a purposeful glint in his blue eyes that sent an icy tingle skittering down Carrie's spine. Then suddenly she realised he was standing right in front of her, effectively shielding her from anyone who came into the room.

Startled by his sudden proximity, she stared up at him with wide eyes. At five foot eight inches she was tall, but even with the added height of Lulu's four-inch stiletto-heeled sandals she had to tip her head back to look at him.

The expression on his face made her heart beat erratically. His glittering blue eyes darkened, and he looked so deeply into her eyes that it felt as if he could see right into her soul. Then he tipped his head slightly to one side, as if he was about to kiss her!

'So lovely,' he murmured, resting his hands gently on the bare skin of her upper arms.

Carrie was transfixed. She simply couldn't tear her gaze away from his face. He was absolutely gorgeous. Everything about his features seemed perfect, from the deep blue eyes fringed with sinfully long lashes to the wide, expressive mouth. And he was looking at her and seeing a desirable woman.

Suddenly she became aware of the sensuous slide of his hand down her arm, skimming lightly over her skin in a way that made the hairs stand up and goosebumps prickle over her exposed flesh. His hand closed over the phone, taking it from her grasp, then in the next second his other arm moved around her, pulling her hard against his muscular frame.

She gasped as her body bumped against his, the skimpy dress doing nothing to shield her from the hot-blooded strength of his powerful masculine form. Her heart was beating so loudly it blocked out all other sounds, and her stomach was turning somersaults. What was he going to do now? He couldn't really mean to kiss her, could he? He didn't even know her!

Somewhere deep inside her mind a tiny rational thought told her to push him off, to back away and get out of there while she still could. But her body was ignoring the niggle of common sense, overriding her instinct for self-preservation. She simply didn't want to do the sensible thing.

She stared up at him, unable to speak or move. Then the moment of no return passed and his mouth came down on hers.

The sensual movement of his lips against hers set her body trembling, and she clung to him, utterly lost in the moment.

Her legs felt weak, and her arms seemed to slide around his broad shoulders of their own volition as she felt her body meld itself to his. He placed one strong hand between her shoulder blades to support her, and by leaning forward pushed her back over the desk. A moment later his other hand found her waist and tugged her tightly to him.

Her hips were pressed against his, and her spine was arched back, pushing her breasts upwards. It was an undeniably erotic position, and a rush of sexual excitement stormed through her body, starting an insistent throbbing of desire deep within her. Then, with unexpected abruptness, he pulled back from the kiss.

She stared at him in startled silence. All she could hear was the sound of her own breathing and the rapid beating of her heart. All she could see was his face, his expression intense but unreadable. He still held her close, but not so tightly as before.

'Carrie?' A man's voice coming from behind the stranger broke through into her awareness. 'I didn't know you were coming this evening.'

Darren! She'd forgotten all about him. Suddenly she remembered she'd taken his mobile phone—then an instant later realised it was no longer in her hand.

'Lulu…Lulu asked me to stay for the party,' she stammered distractedly, hardly able to tear her gaze away from the stranger's face to glance at Darren.

'What are you doing in here?' There was a hint of suspicion colouring his voice as he looked down at his jacket. It was lying rather haphazardly on the chair where Carrie had dropped it. 'Well, I can see *what* you're doing—but why are you doing it in my study?' he added.

'I needed a moment alone with Carrie.' The stranger suddenly spoke, turning his head to look at Darren. From the calm assurance and air of authority he exuded, anyone would think it was his study rather than Darren's.

Carrie's eyes opened wide with shock. How did he know her name—was he simply repeating what he'd just heard Darren call her? And why had he said he wanted to be alone with her? An uncomfortable mixture of emotions rattled through her as she stared at his strong profile. Had he simply followed her into the room with the intention of making a pass at her?

'Nik!' Darren exclaimed. 'Long time no see. You didn't tell me you were coming.'

Carrie frowned in confusion. For some reason she was surprised that Darren knew the stranger, but after all this was his party, and all the people here were his guests. And he'd called the stranger by name—Nik.

'It was a last-minute decision,' Nik said. 'I've just come straight from the airport.'

'I can see you didn't waste any time getting straight down to business, you old dog!' Darren laughed, slapping him soundly on the back. The action bumped Nik hard into Carrie, sending shockwaves of desire ricocheting through her sensitised body. 'And, Carrie,' he added approvingly, 'you dark horse!'

With another jolt she realised that she was still almost indecently entwined with the stranger. His muscled leg was pressing intimately between her thighs, pulling the fabric of her dress taut across her hips and causing it to ride up even higher.

'Well, don't let me interrupt you, mate.' Darren spoke to

Nik as leant past them to pick up his jacket. 'I can see you've got things to do,' he added with a knowing grin as he pulled the mobile phone out of the pocket. 'I've got a phone call to make, so I'll leave you to it. Lock the room if you want,' he finished, closing the door behind him as he left the study.

Carrie stared after him with her mind spinning, then turned back to look into Nik's face, which was still only inches from her own. She was confused and embarrassed by her response to his kiss, but she was also angry with him for putting her in that position in the first place.

'What on earth do you think you were doing?' she demanded, pushing him away from her. She stood up straight, wobbling slightly on her high heels before she found her balance, but then she planted her hands firmly on her hips and stared at him indignantly.

'I would have thought it was obvious,' he drawled, looking completely unmoved as he straightened his tie and tugged at the cuffs of his shirt so that once again he looked immaculate. 'I was replacing the stolen phone, of course.'

'Oh!' Carrie was completely thrown. How could he be so matter-of-fact about what had just happened between them? Had he really only kissed her to provide a distraction while he put the phone back?

The kiss had lasted only moments, but it had had a profound impact on her both physically and mentally. For half a year her identity as an individual with hopes and desires had been locked away. She hadn't thought of herself as a woman with natural needs and passions. Now she had suddenly let go, in a way that even shocked herself.

She'd been so wrapped up in the kiss that she'd been totally oblivious to what was going on around her. Nik, on the other hand, seemed completely unaffected by the experience, and had even been able to concentrate on an entirely different agenda.

He'd simply been creating a smokescreen so Darren wouldn't notice him putting the phone back in his jacket pocket.

'I thought you'd be grateful,' he said, his sensual lips curving up in evident amusement at her obvious confusion and discomfort. 'In fact, I got the impression you rather enjoyed it.'

'I didn't enjoy it!' Carrie felt her cheeks blazing at her barefaced lie. 'And you certainly didn't need to kiss me like that!' she added.

'It's what they always do in the movies. I had to bend you back like that to reach the jacket,' Nik said, with a smile that didn't reach his eyes. 'Besides, you looked like a frightened little rabbit. If I'd stuck out my leg and tripped Darren up, I doubt that you would've had the wit to use the diversion to put his phone back unnoticed.'

'I didn't ask you to help me,' she said, suddenly riled by Nik's casual insult, and by the way he was treating the whole thing as a joke. 'I would have simply explained to Darren that Lulu needed the phone.'

'I'm not going to apologise for kissing you, if that's what you're angling for,' he said. 'I did what I thought was necessary at the time, and that's all there is to it. I wasn't exactly delighted with the situation myself, but I'm not asking for your apologies.'

'I've got nothing to say sorry for!' Carrie protested, her emotions see-sawing horribly. She'd found the kiss totally mind-blowing, yet Nik apparently had a very different view of the whole thing. 'I didn't ask you to kiss me. It's not my fault you found it so awful!'

'I wasn't talking about the kiss, of course. Why are women always so insecure about these things?' he asked, with an exaggerated lift of his eyebrows. 'I meant that I wasn't thrilled to discover you're a thief. I'd hoped that you were a reasonable, honest person.'

'What?' she gasped, struggling to understand the implication of his words. Why did he care what sort of person she was? Suddenly she remembered him telling Darren that he needed a moment alone with her. Who *was* he?

'First impressions count for a lot,' he continued, letting his gaze drift slowly down her body, lingering meaningfully on the fullness of her breasts before skimming down to her narrow waist.

'Who are you?' She held herself straight and refused to fidget under his blatant scrutiny. 'And what do you want from me?'

He didn't answer immediately, and, still not making eye contact, rudely let his gaze sweep lower, moving over the swell of her hips and down her long exposed legs to the tips of her toes. She was just about to repeat her question when his eyes snapped up to meet hers.

'My name is Nikos Kristallis,' he said coldly. 'And I have come to discuss arrangements for my nephew.'

CHAPTER TWO

CARRIE couldn't speak. She was so shocked she could hardly think.

She simply stared at him. Nikos Kristallis. He was the younger brother of Sophie's husband, Leonidas. The favoured son of the proud and arrogant Cosmo Kristallis. He was Danny's uncle.

A nasty sensation of dread settled in her stomach, but she took a deep breath to steady herself. She tried not to think about her distressing encounter with Cosmo Kristallis at the funeral, which suddenly loomed up in the front of her mind. It had been a horrible experience, and her memories of the occasion were inseparable from the soul-wrenching grief for her loved ones.

'What are you doing here?' When she finally managed to speak, her voice was no more than a scratchy whisper.

Nik watched the profound impact of his words on Carrie Thomas with a strange sense of satisfaction. The colour drained from her face with startling speed and for a moment she appeared totally stunned.

He was pleased. Not that he liked to inflict pain on people as a general rule, but Carrie Thomas was different. She had taken something that belonged to him, and he would do whatever it took to get it back!

'I have come to discuss my nephew,' Nik replied. 'Now I have identified myself to you, I would have thought that was obvious.'

'I have nothing to say to you about Danny,' Carrie said. Her face was very white against her black hair, but the spark was suddenly back in her green eyes. 'We have nothing to discuss.' She stalked across to the door and walked out.

Nik made no attempt to stop her leaving.

It suited him to get her away from the crowds at this footballer's party. It was too public for what he had to do, and there were definitely too many photographers about.

Nik's eyes narrowed as he watched Carrie weave her way through the crowds of partygoers. She was a gorgeous creature. His investigators had provided him with photos, so he'd known she would be attractive, but those photos had done nothing to reveal the incredible full-blooded impact of her presence.

She was making rapid progress across the room, stepping lightly in her strappy sandals, the extraordinary height of the heels creating a delicious tension in her shapely legs. Every man present was looking at her as she passed. Every man present was picturing those long, long legs wrapped around him. Or maybe it was just Nik. Certainly he couldn't shake the thought of kissing her again. Kissing her and more, much more.

Her silky black hair hung loose past her shoulders, swinging alluringly in time with her step. He wanted to slip his hands under that shimmering black curtain and brush it aside to expose the naked skin of her back, to reveal the zip that ran skin-tight down her spine.

He imagined easing that zip down and running his hands all over that sexy body, teasing and caressing her, removing all her clothes until she was naked and ready for him. He knew she wouldn't be a passive lover. He longed to look deep into those green eyes as she writhed beneath him, as he took her to the brink of ecstasy.

Suddenly he realised she was almost at the door. Pushing his erotic thoughts about her aside, he stirred himself to follow. He knew where she was going, but it would be wise to keep her in his sights.

Carrie picked up her denim jacket and sporty backpack from an alcove by the front door, then stopped and scanned the room for Lulu. She was desperate to get out of there, but she couldn't forget about her friend—especially when she had been so upset earlier. She spotted her almost immediately, hurrying down the staircase looking determined, in freshly applied make-up and dressed to kill in a slinky silver cocktail dress.

'I'm really sorry,' Carrie said, as soon as Lulu reached her. 'I couldn't get the phone.'

'Don't worry about it,' Lulu said, sounding remarkably calm considering her previous histrionics. She was looking across at Darren, who was talking and joking with a group of men. 'I'll get it myself. He can't have listened to the message yet, or he wouldn't be looking so happy.'

Then, without another word for Carrie, she walked across the room towards her husband. Carrie looked after Lulu for a moment, hoping everything would turn out all right, but she couldn't stay any longer. Apart from her desire to get as far away from Nikos Kristallis as possible, she had to hurry—because she was already late picking up Danny. She turned and left through the front door.

The blast of cool air on her face felt good, and she took a deep breath as she hurried down the marble steps of the swanky London town house to the street below.

It was a relief to be out of there, away from the piercing gaze of Nikos Kristallis. She'd felt his eyes burning a hole in her back all the way across the room. She shivered, imagining the predatory intensity in his expression as he'd watched her walking away from him.

She set off down the street quickly, her heels clicking on the pavement as she walked. Her fingers were surprisingly shaky as she buttoned up her denim jacket, and she had to resist the urge to look behind her to see if Nikos Kristallis had also left the party.

Why was he in London? Had he come to finish off what his father had started at the funeral? Maybe he wanted her to sign legal documents saying she would never pursue a connection with the Kristallis family?

She shook herself sharply and forced herself to put it all out of her mind for now. She couldn't be upset when she picked up Danny. It wouldn't be fair on him.

It was a long walk to his nursery, but with any luck she'd be able to hail a black cab. She turned the corner onto the main road and, amazingly, the first taxi she tried for pulled over. She gave the driver directions and climbed inside, suddenly uncomfortably aware of his eyes on her exposed legs. No wonder she'd got a cab so easily.

A few minutes later she paid the driver and jumped out into the crowd of London commuters hurrying along the pavement. She ducked into a doorway and pressed the buzzer.

'It's Carrie Thomas,' she said into the metal grille. 'I'm so sorry I'm late.'

With a long low buzz the lock released and she was into the building. Up one flight of stairs, and another security door later she was into Danny's nursery.

'Danny!' she cried, dashing over and picking the baby up.

Tears suddenly pricked in her eyes. It felt wonderful to hug him tight. She was sure she couldn't love him any more than she did, even if he was her own son.

Nikos Kristallis had wasted his time coming to London.

Leonidas had always said he never wanted Danny to have anything to do with his Greek family. He had even made Sophie promise that if anything ever happened to him she'd never let them get their hands on him. Now, after meeting Cosmo and Nik, it was easy for Carrie to understand his reasons. And the least she could do for Sophie was to keep the promise she'd made to her husband before they were killed.

'Sorry I'm late,' she said, kissing the top of Danny's head and looking over his tousled brown hair into the face of the nursery assistant who had been sharing a picture book with him.

'That's all right,' the girl said. 'We've been having a nice story—haven't we, Danny?'

'You'll find the penalty for a late pick-up added to your bill, Miss Thomas.'

Carrie winced at the sound of the nursery manager's voice, but she plastered a smile onto her face before she looked round. She could hardly afford the nursery bill as it was.

'I'm sorry, Mrs Plewman,' she said. 'I got held up.'

'Hmm.' Mrs Plewman was unimpressed, making no attempt to hide her disapproval as she took in the short skirt of the sparkly red dress and the high-heeled sandals Carrie was still wearing. It was lucky she'd buttoned her denim jacket up to hide the low-cut front. 'I'm not running a charity here, Miss Thomas. Make sure it doesn't happen again. I've got my staff to think about, you know, but I'll waive the penalty payment just this once.'

'Thank you very much, Mrs Plewman. Have a nice evening.' Carrie swung Danny's bag onto her back, along with her own backpack, and retrieved his buggy from the cupboard in the hallway. She couldn't wait to get home, to the safety and comfort of her flat.

Nik stood outside the building, frowning as an unexpected knot of anticipation twisted deep inside his gut. It was an unfamiliar sensation. He was about to lay eyes on his orphaned nephew for the first time—but why should that make him feel so unsettled?

He'd tried to picture the baby, but he just couldn't imagine what he was going to look like. He must have seen hundreds of babies in his life, but he'd never really looked at one properly. It would be very strange, returning to Greece with a child.

At last he saw Carrie Thomas emerge from the building, a dark-haired baby balanced on her hip and a folded buggy in her other hand. She glanced up and down the street, but the crowds of passing commuters hid him from her view.

His eyes fixed on the baby, his dead brother's son, and a peculiar numbness crept over him. That baby was his family. That baby was all his estranged brother Leonidas had left behind.

He started walking mechanically across the wide London pavement towards them, watching Carrie open the buggy with a practised flick of her wrist and snap the safety catch into place with her foot. All the time she was holding the baby tightly, engaging his attention with a constant stream of chatter and smiles.

'In you go, Danny,' she said, securing the child in the seat with the harness. 'Off we go—tube or bus? What do you think?' She glanced down the street at the queue by the bus stop.

'We still need to talk,' Nik said, coming up beside her.

She gasped in surprise. But the change in her body language made him sure she had recognised his voice before she looked round.

'Anyone would think you were stalking me!' She flicked her silky black fringe out of her eyes as she turned to him.

Nik looked down at her upturned face. Her almond-shaped eyes were a dazzling green, framed by arching brows and accentuated by long black lashes. He saw no sign of any make-up, and her flawless skin was incredibly pale, but it was lit somehow by a shimmering vitality.

It suddenly struck him as odd that she wasn't wearing any make-up. Surely that natural look didn't usually accompany the style of outfit she was wearing? But then, the denim jacket buttoned up to her chin and the sporty backpack seemed somewhat incongruous, too.

'You left before we finished our conversation,' Nik said.

'I don't have anything to say to you,' Carrie said. She looked so cool, standing there, but he knew from experience that her nubile body was anything but.

'Really?' Nik asked coldly. 'Tell me, why did you steal my brother's baby?'

'I… I…' Carrie stammered. She gripped the handles of the buggy tightly and took a step backwards across the pavement. 'I didn't *steal* Danny.'

She stared at him with wide, frightened eyes, suddenly looking even paler than before, if that was possible. She looked genuinely shocked by his words. Maybe she hadn't expected him to cut to the chase so quickly.

'What else would you call taking a baby that doesn't belong to you?' Nik asked. She couldn't really be surprised by his question, could she? In a moment she'd probably recover herself and start spouting a prepared speech in her defence.

'Babies don't belong *to* people!' Carrie gasped. 'They belong *with* the people who love them.'

'They belong with their family,' Nik said, hearing an edge of menace in his own voice as he took a step closer to her. 'And, like I said, you stole that baby from his family.'

'I didn't steal Danny,' Carrie said. 'When his parents were killed in the accident no one else wanted him.'

'No one else was given the chance,' Nik said.

'Your father—'

'My father is dead,' Nik interrupted coldly.

She drew in a sharp breath and stared up at him with puzzled green eyes. He had clearly startled her again, yet as he watched an expression of genuine sympathy passed across her face.

'I'm sorry,' she said. 'I—'

'No.' He cut her off abruptly with an impatient gesture. Her sympathy was the last thing he wanted.

His father had died suddenly just two months ago—four months after Leonidas had been killed in the motorway accident. Nik had had a heavy couple of months, taking over the areas of the family business that his father had still controlled, but things had finally been coming into order when he'd made an astonishing discovery amongst his father's personal papers. Leonidas had left behind an orphaned baby boy.

His gaze dropped to study the baby sitting in the buggy beside him—his brother's son—then he looked back up at the woman who had taken him.

She swallowed convulsively as their eyes met, obviously unnerved by him, and took an awkward step backwards into the crowd of commuters.

'Oi! Watch out!' a young man shouted as he careered into her back, nearly knocking her off her feet. Her stiletto heels didn't help, and she staggered forward, ramming the buggy hard into Nik's shins.

He swore in Greek. 'We need to get off the street,' he grated, hauling Carrie and the buggy sideways, into the relative safety of a café doorway. 'I'll signal my driver.'

'I'm not getting into a car with you.' Carrie shrugged his hand off her arm and bobbed down to check on Danny. 'I hardly know you,' she said, rising to her full heel-enhanced height and meeting his eye.

'We have to talk, and the street is not the place for it,' Nik said categorically. 'We'll go in here.' He indicated the stylish Italian café they were standing beside.

Carrie hesitated, biting her lip as she thought about it. She knew she'd have to talk to Nikos Kristallis some time, and quite honestly she'd rather get it over with.

'All right, but I'm not staying long.' She stooped to lift Danny out of his buggy. 'He'll be getting tired soon.'

A few minutes later they were sitting at a table in a quiet corner at the back of the café. Danny was balanced on Carrie's lap, making alarming lunges for her cappuccino.

She edged her chair away from the table, automatically shifting Danny out of reach of the hot drink, and glanced surreptitiously at Nik. She couldn't let herself believe that he really wanted to take Danny from her. It was six months since she'd contacted his family with news of Leonidas's death, and if Nik had genuinely intended to take Danny he wouldn't have waited so long to seek her out.

She was anxious to know what he really wanted, but she resisted the urge to ask him straight out. She wanted him to put his cards on the table first, to give her a chance to process what he said. But he'd hardly spoken since they'd sat down, and now he sipped his espresso in silence.

She couldn't help letting her eyes run over him, drinking in his amazing good looks. His designer suit hung immaculately on his lean, athletic body, emphasising the powerful width of his shoulders and the strong hard planes of his chest. The crisp white shirt he wore was the perfect foil for his bronzed skin, which glowed with an attractive health and vigour.

'I'm sorry about your father.' She was still wary of Nik, but she couldn't stand sitting in silence any longer. 'It must have been awful to lose him so soon after Leonidas.'

'Thank you for your concern,' Nik said, putting his espresso cup down and lifting cold blue eyes to meet hers.

'But I didn't come here to discuss my recent bereavement. I'm here to make arrangements regarding the child.'

'What do you mean?' A bolt of alarm shot through Carrie, making her heart lurch and her stomach churn unpleasantly.

'Danny belongs in Greece with me.'

Carrie swayed back in her chair, clutching Danny tightly as she stared at Nik in disbelief. It couldn't be true. He didn't really want Danny, did he?

'I'm sorry for your loss,' she said tautly. 'But Danny is staying with me.'

'No,' Nik said. 'Danny will return to Greece with me.'

'I understand you're upset, losing your brother and then your father so soon afterwards,' Carrie said, desperately holding on to her control. She mustn't let him see how upset she was rapidly becoming as the fact that he might be serious about taking Danny away from her started to sink in. 'But you didn't want Danny six months ago. You can't just decide to look after a child when it suits you.'

'Don't insult me,' Nik said, looking at her squarely. 'This isn't about me—it's about Danny's right to be part of his real family.'

'Are you saying I'm not his real family?' Carrie gasped.

'You're not his immediate family,' Nik said. 'And you are clearly not a suitable guardian.'

'What's that supposed to mean?' Carrie was shocked. 'You don't even know me!'

'I know that I caught you stealing,' he said.

'I wasn't stealing,' Carrie protested, thinking about Lulu's plaintive cry for help. She wasn't ashamed of trying to help her friend. It was none of Nik's business, but suddenly she decided to tell him everything. It would be better than having him speculate about what she'd been doing. 'Lulu asked me to do it. She was worried Darren would start a row with her over a message she'd left on his phone, so she wanted to delete it.'

She looked at Nik, to see if he'd accepted her explanation, but his expression was still unreadable.

'I realise it can't have been easy, looking after a baby on your own,' Nik said, abruptly changing the subject back to Danny. 'But—'

'It's been perfectly all right,' Carrie said quickly. 'Wonderful, in fact!' There was no way she'd ever admit how hard she'd found it looking after the baby alone, juggling work commitments and trying to make ends meet financially.

'I'm his uncle,' Nik said flatly. 'You are his cousin.'

'What difference does that make?' Carrie demanded. 'I was there when he needed someone. Nobody else wanted him then. Your father called him a brat…' She hesitated, looking down at the cold grey marble tabletop. She didn't want to remember her horrible meeting with Cosmo Kristallis. It was too hurtful to think about the way Danny's grandfather had viewed him.

'You met my father?' Nik asked sharply. 'When?'

Something in the tone of his voice made Carrie's eyes fly back to his face. A muscle pulsed at his jaw and a line of tension creased his brow.

'He came to the funeral,' Carrie replied carefully. At that moment she felt more than a little afraid of how he might react.

'Last November,' Nik said, after a slight pause.

'Yes.' Carrie looked at him warily, wondering whether talking about his father and brother was painful for him. He hadn't shown any sign of it, but it was impossible to know what was going on behind his implacable expression.

'What did my father say to you?' Nik asked.

'Not much,' Carrie replied cautiously. 'He simply said that he felt it would be in Danny's best interests if he remained in England with his mother's family.'

'Really?' Nik gave a sudden ironic burst of laughter. 'I

knew my father, and I doubt very much that those were his exact words.'

'What your father said wasn't funny.' How could he be laughing at a time like this?

'I'm sure it wasn't.' There was a hard glint in his blue eyes. 'But listening to you putting such measured, almost caring words into his mouth is amusing.'

'Your father didn't care about Danny at all!' Carrie said. 'He wished Danny had never been born!'

'Probably,' said Nik. 'But I do not share his view on that.'

'If that's the case, where were you after the accident? You didn't care enough to come then!' She was so upset that she didn't realise her voice was rising. Suddenly Danny made another lunge for her cappuccino.

'Careful, Danny!' She pulled him back, but in her haste her own elbow caught against the cup. It rattled in the saucer, and a moment later the table was awash with foamy coffee.

She jumped to her feet to avoid the flood of coffee, quickly checking none of the scalding liquid had come anywhere near Danny.

'Hot drinks and babies—not a good combination,' Nik remarked smoothly. He turned and lifted a commanding hand to catch the attention of the girl behind the counter. 'We need a cloth here.'

Carrie hugged Danny and looked at the mess she'd made. Nik had got her so upset that she hardly knew what to think or say. She dabbed her paper napkin into the flood of liquid, but it was saturated in a second, and it didn't stop the coffee running off the marble tabletop onto the café floor.

'I have to go.' She bent to pick up her bag, barely registering that it was sitting in a pool of coffee, and turned to retrieve the buggy—but Nik was already holding it. 'I'm really sorry about the mess,' she said, as the waitress appeared with a large cloth.

She turned and made her way outside.

'We haven't finished this conversation yet,' Nik said, joining her back on the busy London pavement.

'Yes, we have.' She tugged the buggy away from him before he could react. 'I'm taking Danny home.'

'I'll drive you,' Nik said.

'No, thank you.' She glanced up the road, and relief washed over her as she saw a bus approaching. 'Here's my bus now. Danny likes the bus.'

Without waiting for a reply she hoisted the buggy up under her arm and, hanging on to Danny tightly, made a dash for the bus stop.

He laughed, and settled on her lap happily as the bus pulled away. Out of the corner of her eye Carrie could still see Nik, standing on the pavement. She stared straight ahead, resisting the urge to look. A shiver ran down her spine as the bus rumbled to a halt alongside him.

It was true that Danny liked the bus, but she could think of many nicer things than sitting cramped, with a buggy gripped awkwardly between her knees, trying to keep a wriggling baby out of the damp patch of coffee on her short red dress, all the while knowing that those piercing Greek eyes were fixed on her from behind the grimy window of a London bus.

She knew she should have stayed longer—to find out exactly how serious Nikos Kristallis was about taking Danny. But right now all she wanted was to be as far away from him as possible.

Nik watched the bus labouring through the heavy traffic. He knew that Carrie was aware of him, standing there, but she was looking forward, refusing to acknowledge his presence.

It was only a couple of hours since he'd met her, but already Carrie Thomas had become strangely significant in his life. She had known Leonidas while he'd been lost to Nik. She'd even met his father. And now she had his nephew.

Nik saw that Danny had spotted him standing there. He had no hesitation at all in staring right back at Nik. His bright button eyes were fixed on him, and he turned his head and leant forward to keep him in view as long as possible when the bus finally moved off into the stream of traffic.

That baby boy was all that was left of Leonidas. Carrie Thomas could take the child home tonight, but it wouldn't be long before he was taking him home to Greece.

CHAPTER THREE

CARRIE hurried along the street towards Danny's nursery. It had been an exhausting day, and all she could think about was collecting Danny and taking him safely back to the refuge of her flat. Normally she loved her work, but she was so tired and stressed, after a sleepless night worrying about what Nikos Kristallis meant to do, that the day had seemed endless.

She told herself that Nik didn't really mean to take Danny away from her. After all, if he was genuinely interested in Danny, surely he would have made an appearance before now? And even if he really did want Danny, he couldn't just take him. He might be rich and powerful, but he would still have to make arrangements through the proper channels—otherwise it would be kidnapping.

She was starting to regret leaving the previous evening before anything had been resolved. Not knowing Nik's intentions was killing her, and she'd been on edge all day, half expecting Nik to contact her at any moment. Every time the phone had rung she'd nearly jumped out of her skin. Her thoughts had kept turning to Danny, and how much she loved him, and by the end of the afternoon her nerves had been in shreds. Now, as she made her way quickly through the crowds of commuters hurrying along the street, she was desperate to reach Danny and wrap him safely in her arms.

Suddenly she stopped in her tracks. She stared across the wide London street, momentarily unable to believe what she saw.

Nikos Kristallis was standing on the doorstep of Danny's nursery, leaning forward slightly as if he was talking into the intercom.

Buses and taxis flashed across her line of vision, making it hard to see clearly. She couldn't be right. She was so stressed her eyes were playing tricks on her.

No, it was real. The heavy door was swinging closed behind Nikos Kristallis, but just before it slammed shut she saw him heading swiftly up the stairs. He was going to take Danny!

Carrie's heart thudded in her chest and she broke into a run, weaving in and out of people as she sprinted along the pavement towards the crossing. The lights were just changing from red to amber, and four lanes of traffic started revving up as the last pedestrians cleared the road. She dashed out anyway, ignoring the angry shouts and blaring horns as she focussed on the nursery door. If Nik came back out carrying Danny she had to reach him quickly. She could not lose him in the crowd.

She skidded to a halt at the doorway and pressed impatiently on the buzzer, panting for breath.

'It's Carrie Thomas!' she gasped. 'Please let me in.'

She was already leaning heavily on the door, and the instant the lock released she was through, bounding up the stairs two at a time. She couldn't let Nikos Kristallis get to Danny.

She burst through the door at the top of the stairs and dashed along the corridor to the baby room. Danny was there on the play mat—safe and sound.

She called his name and he looked round, but the moment his eyes found her his little face crumpled into tears.

'Up you come, poppet,' the young nursery assistant said, picking him up before Carrie was able to unlatch the child safety gate and get into the room. 'He hasn't been himself today,' she continued, speaking to Carrie. 'Been a bit grizzly all day. I think he might be teething.'

'Poor little thing,' Carrie said, holding out her arms to take Danny from the young woman. She hugged him tightly, feeling some of her anxiety ease as she pressed her face against his hair. Then she held him away from her and looked at him carefully. His cheeks were flushed, but he had already stopped crying.

Voices coming along the corridor suddenly caught her attention, and she remembered with a sick feeling that Nikos Kristallis was in the building.

'And this is our baby unit,' she heard Mrs Plewman saying right behind her. 'It has excellent facilities, and most importantly one member of staff for every two babies.'

Carrie turned on the spot and found herself staring up into the face of Nikos Kristallis. He looked completely indifferent to the fact that she had discovered him at the nursery—a place he had no reasonable reason to be—and her concern over his presence suddenly switched to anger. He was so arrogant that he thought normal rules didn't apply to him.

'What are you doing here?' She rounded on him. 'You have no right to be anywhere near Danny!'

'Mrs Plewman has been kind enough to give me a tour of the nursery,' he replied smoothly, throwing the nursery manager a charming smile.

'I don't want this man anywhere near Danny.' She spoke urgently to Mrs Plewman. 'I don't trust him—he wants to take Danny away, back to Greece with him.'

'I have a right to see where my nephew is being cared for,' Nik replied.

'But that's not why you're here,' Carrie said, hugging Danny protectively and glaring up at him.

'Your nephew?' Mrs Plewman said. Her deferential manner indicated that up until that point she had been impressed by Nik, but now Carrie's reaction had given her pause for thought.

'Yes, Danny is my nephew,' Nik confirmed, but his sharp blue eyes were fixed on Carrie. 'What other reason have I got to come here?'

'To take Danny,' Carrie said. 'To get your hands on him when I'm not around.'

'You really are overreacting,' Nik said with infuriating blandness. 'As Mrs Plewman will tell you, unauthorised people are not permitted to collect the children left in her care. And, quite apart from that, if that was my intention why would I choose to come at the exact time you are due to arrive?'

'So that the staff see us together? To make yourself seem familiar? To give you credibility?' Carrie rattled off the first things that came into her mind.

'Being seen with you would give me *credibility*?' Nik repeated. His eyes swept across her disparagingly, and his disdainful expression made it all too clear what he thought of that idea.

'I'm taking Danny home now,' Carrie said stiffly. 'And just to be sure you understand—you are not to come here again. In fact, I don't want you bothering us at all.'

Carrie didn't wait for a reply. She knew she ought to talk to Mrs Plewman properly, to make it absolutely clear that no one but her should ever collect Danny. But at that moment she simply had to get away.

She let the door swing shut as she walked through and bent to pull the buggy out of the cupboard. Suddenly Nik was beside her again, taking it out of her hand.

'Let me,' he said. 'It's rather dangerous to carry so much on the stairs at once.'

'I've got it, thank you,' Carrie snapped, reaching out for the buggy.

'I'm here, and I can help,' Nik said firmly. 'What's the point of needlessly risking your neck, and more importantly my nephew's neck, when you don't have to?'

'I'm not risking anyone's neck,' Carrie said, but she turned and started down the stairs. The sooner she got outside, the sooner she could catch the bus home.

'I'll give you a lift home,' Nik said, once they'd stepped out onto the street.

'Are you mad?' Carrie gasped, pulling the buggy out of his grasp and flicking it open with an angry gesture that revealed all her pent-up emotions. 'I'm not going anywhere with you!'

'We still have to talk,' Nik replied. 'You ran off before we'd finished yesterday. I know when you collect Danny, and it seemed an appropriate time and place to meet.'

'You had no right to go into his nursery.' Carrie hugged the one-year-old protectively. 'And Mrs Plewman had no business letting you in!' She knew that wasn't exactly fair to the nursery manager. But even as she tried to reassure herself that Mrs Plewman would never have let a stranger take Danny a shiver ran down her spine. Nik had clearly been doing an excellent job of charming her. There was no way to tell what would have happened if Carrie hadn't arrived when she had.

'My nephew has no business being in that appalling place,' Nik replied. 'I wanted to see for myself what kind of care he's been receiving, and frankly I was not impressed. He will certainly not be spending any more time in that dreadful environment. That is not the way a Kristallis child is cared for.'

'His name may be Kristallis,' Carrie said, bristling at his harsh judgement of the nursery she had so carefully chosen for Danny. 'But Sophie and Leonidas didn't want him brought up like a Kristallis.'

'His parents are dead. He is my responsibility now,' Nik stated, his expression hard and unreadable.

'Now? He's nearly one!' Carrie exclaimed. 'How very responsible of you to miss the first year of his life!'

She knew she had hit a nerve the second the words were out of her mouth.

A change came over Nik so profound it made her blood suddenly run cold.

'I don't intend to miss any more of his life,' Nik grated. 'Now, we need to find somewhere to talk.'

'Danny needs to go home.' Carrie looked at his flushed face and smoothed his hair back from his forehead. It felt uncomfortably warm. 'It's not fair to keep him out if he's feeling under the weather.'

'Then I'll give you a lift home.' Nik indicated a sleek black limousine that was just pulling up next to the pavement. 'When the child is settled, we can talk.'

'I don't need a lift, thank you,' Carrie said. 'We'll be perfectly all right on the bus, just the same as every other day.'

'Don't be ridiculous,' Nik said. 'Just because you seem to have taken an irrational dislike to me, it doesn't mean my nephew has to suffer the unnecessary discomfort of a public bus.'

'There's nothing wrong with buses. Not everyone has a private limo, you know.' She glanced down and caught sight of her reflection in the tinted window of the long black car.

Suddenly she remembered seeing Nik going in to the nursery. If he had taken Danny and put him into that car she might never have seen him again. They could have driven right past her and she'd never have known Danny was hidden from view behind that sinister dark glass. 'I'm not getting into a car with you. I hardly know you.'

'The child doesn't look well,' Nik said. 'Don't let your pride and petty dislike of me make you ignore what is best for Danny.'

'He's not sick.' Carrie bit her lip as she studied Danny and pressed her hand against his face again. 'Teething can make babies hot and bothered, but it doesn't mean he's sick.'

Just at that moment the heavens opened, and it began to pour with rain. Danny howled as the first huge drops started to splash his face, and Carrie looked around in dismay. Rush hour was in full swing, and the thought of a crowded bus or tube train full of disgruntled commuters with dripping umbrellas, jostling her and tripping over Danny's buggy, was simply awful.

But she couldn't accept a lift with Nik. It was true that she hardly knew him, and she was still suspicious as to his motives for going into the nursery. Then Danny began to cry more loudly, and when she touched his cheek to soothe him it felt even hotter. She really ought to get him home quickly.

'I'm giving you a lift home whether you like it or not. Tell my driver where you live.'

Despite her protestations Nik swept Danny out of her arms and stooped to secure him in a child's car seat, which was already in position in the back of the limousine. Carrie bit her lip, wondering what to do. It was pouring with rain and Danny needed to get home. She'd be with him all the time in the limousine, and it would be a lot quicker than the bus.

The driver had the buggy and was struggling to fold it. Carrie took it from him and collapsed it down with a couple of swift and practised gestures. She didn't want the driver to pinch his fingers. Though if it had been Nik trying to fold it that would have been a different matter.

A minute later she was riding in comfort in the back of the luxury limousine with Nik. Danny was crying at the top of his lungs, and nothing she did seemed to make him feel any better.

The nursery staff had thought Danny was teething. They had years of experience with babies and always seemed to know what they were talking about. But Carrie was beginning to worry that Danny might be ill. He really didn't look right. But then it had probably been unsettling for him to see her arguing with Nik.

'You shouldn't have gone into the nursery.' Carrie spoke suddenly. 'You should have waited for me. You knew I'd only be a couple of minutes.'

'You wouldn't have taken me inside,' Nik replied. 'I didn't like seeing him in that place, being cared for by strangers,' he added. 'He should be looked after by family.'

'Those people aren't strangers to Danny,' Carrie said, pulling a toy out of her bag and trying in vain to cheer the baby up. 'The nursery might be a bit old and shabby, but I chose it because you can tell that the staff really love the children. Also, they have a fantastic ratio of staff to children—much better than any of the other places I looked at.'

'It's not the same as being with his family,' Nik insisted.

'You may be a blood relation to Danny,' Carrie said, 'but you're the stranger to him—not the nursery ladies.'

'That's something that's going to change,' Nik said.

Carrie looked at him sharply. Something in his tone of voice made her nervous. The nursery didn't seem such a safe place any more—how could she know it was safe to leave Danny there when she had to work?

Suddenly Danny upped the volume of his wailing, and all her attention flipped back to him. Poor child. She couldn't bear to think of him sick. And if he was poorly, rather than teething, she wouldn't be able to travel with him to Spain tomorrow with a client. She hated letting anyone down, especially a valued friend and client like Elaine, but Danny was more important than anything else.

'Here.' Nik picked up a bag of baby toys and handed them to Carrie.

She took the bag and pulled out a colourful rattle that seemed to be battery operated, with flashing lights and music. Danny usually enjoyed noisy toys.

To Carrie's relief, after a last couple of sobs he fell silent, reached out a chubby little hand and took the rattle. She pushed the 'on' button, starting the flashing and music.

Danny began howling instantly.

'Maybe not the best choice of toy.' A patronising edge to Nik's voice set Carrie's nerves on edge. 'I don't imagine all that noise and flashing is very good if he has a headache.'

Carrie gritted her teeth and leant forward to switch off the wretched device. Danny wasn't the only one with a headache. She could feel the tension starting to clamp round her head and shoulders like a steel vice.

'There's no "off" switch!' she said in exasperation. 'Oh! I hate noisy toys you can't stop once they've started.'

'I'm sure he'll enjoy it when he's feeling better.' Nik was infuriatingly calm as he bent forward and studied Danny.

His face was only a few inches away from Danny's and although he wasn't doing anything but looking intently at the baby he seemed to catch his attention. The baby stopped crying, and while he didn't look exactly happy, he wasn't getting himself into a frenzy any more.

Carrie tried to ignore the feeling of foreboding that crept over her as she watched Nik and Danny staring at each other. The sudden silence as the musical rattle finally reached the end of its song seemed horribly ominous.

'Danny can't go back to that place.' Nik spoke without turning to look at her, but that didn't weaken the impact of his words.

'He has to—so I can go to work.' Carrie had to earn a living. It was as simple as that. She straightened her shoulders, refusing to let herself be intimidated by Nikos Kristallis and his self-important attitude.

'What happened to the rest of your family?' he asked.

The question caught her off-guard. For some reason she had assumed he knew all about how she had ended up alone with Danny.

'My mother died when I was very young.' She spoke steadily, knowing it was best to be open with him, but she was determined not to let any emotion show in her voice. She didn't need to lay her heartfelt feelings out for him to scrutinise.

'And your father?' he prompted.

'My father couldn't cope.' She thought unhappily how he hadn't even managed to come to the funeral six months ago. 'He left me with my aunt and uncle and their daughter, Sophie.'

'And you grew up as part of their family?'

'Sophie was like a sister to me.' Tears suddenly pricked in Carrie's eyes and she dropped her gaze slightly, determined not to let Nik see. Her relationship with her aunt and uncle had never been warm. Somehow the infrequent but unsettling appearances of her father bringing them money for her upkeep had seen to that. But she had loved Sophie.

'You lost a great deal in that car accident.'

Something in Nik's voice made her look up. Their eyes met and a tremor ran through her. For a long moment she couldn't look away, despite the knowledge that he'd seen the tears swimming in her eyes.

Then Danny made a sound, and suddenly the spell was broken.

She looked back at the baby, and the love she felt for him welled up inside her. She wouldn't let Nik take him from her. She couldn't be parted from Danny now.

She'd loved him from the moment she saw him, and had revelled in their time together since then—even though hardly anyone had been truly supportive about her decision to take on an orphaned baby. Sometimes it felt as if they were all watching her, waiting to see how she would perform.

Her friends from the small town where she had grown up kept telling her to return home, where there were people who could help her out if she needed it. They told her it was irresponsible to try bringing up a baby alone in the city, especially as she had no experience and no one to help her. But Carrie had worked very hard to escape her painful roots, and she'd do almost anything to avoid going back.

She'd made a very different life for herself in London. She had been enjoying her new lifestyle, and found a real sense of achievement from her increasingly successful career as a personal trainer. Her London friends knew nothing about her childhood, and that was how she wanted it, but it meant they had no way to understand why looking after her orphaned cousin was so important to her.

Danny looked a bit better now. His cheeks were still flushed, and his wispy brown fringe was sticking damply to his forehead, but for the moment he was all right. They'd be home very soon, and she had to admit—to herself, anyway—that this way of travelling was better for a grizzly child than crowded, unreliable public transport.

Looking at Danny, comfy and secure in the car seat, she suddenly wondered why Nik had a car seat in his limousine. The thought that he might be married with children made her stomach lurch. Surely a family man wanting to adopt his nephew would have a better chance in court than a bachelor businessman?

'Do you and your wife have children?' Carrie asked abruptly.

'Why do you ask?' Nik said, the expression on his face telling Carrie he had misinterpreted her interest.

'You have a car seat,' she said flatly. She had no intention of letting him see how much the meaningful gleam in his eyes had suddenly made her heart beat faster. No doubt Nikos

Kristallis was used to women throwing themselves at him—but she had more to think about than just herself.

He might be the most gorgeous man she'd ever seen, and there was no question that she had found him overwhelmingly attractive at first, but that had been before she'd learned his identity. That kiss in Darren's study had been extraordinary for her—she was inexperienced and had had no idea a kiss could affect her so profoundly—but at that point she hadn't discovered the threat he posed to her and Danny.

'I am not married, and do not at present have children.' Nik spoke smoothly, but his deep blue eyes were narrowed and fixed on her altogether too sharply. 'However, we can continue our discussion about my marital status later.'

'I thought the discussion was already finished.' The last thing Carrie wanted was for Nikos Kristallis to start getting ideas. Or, even worse, to think that she was getting ideas! 'Your marital status is of no interest to me,' she added quickly.

'Really?' Nik drawled, 'I thought you asked for a reason—a more pressing one than why I have a child's car seat in my limousine.'

'What possible reason could I have?' she replied. 'I was just making conversation.'

Nik smiled. It was a supercilious smile, with an infuriating lift to his straight black eyebrows. She turned to look out through the tinted window at the rainy street outside the limousine, and was desperately trying to think of a suitably cutting remark to put him in his place when his sudden movement towards Danny took her by surprise.

'What are you doing? Don't undo his seatbelt—it isn't safe!' she gasped.

'How else will we take him inside?' Nik sounded genuinely surprised. 'I assume that my driver has brought us to the correct address.'

Carrie realised with a shock that the limousine had stopped moving. She glanced back through the tinted glass of the window and saw that the street she had been looking at was her own! They were parked outside her home.

'Thank you for the ride,' she said, trying to sound cool even though she suddenly felt very silly. 'I'll take Danny now.'

'All right,' Nik said. 'I'll bring your things.'

A gust of cold rainy wind blew into the limousine as the driver opened her door. She lifted Danny up, slid across the black leather seat, and stepped out onto the wet pavement.

'Thank you very much,' she said to the driver.

'We need to get Danny inside, where it's warm and dry,' Nik said. 'Then we can decide on the best thing to do—whether he needs to see a doctor or—'

'*We?*' Carrie echoed, her hackles instantly rising at his arrogant assumption that he was coming inside with her to decide what was best for Danny. She was his guardian. Nikos Kristallis didn't even know him. '*I'll* take him inside,' she said firmly. 'There's no need for you to go to any more trouble. Thank you for your help,' she added, in a voice she knew didn't sound convincingly grateful.

She reached out to take the pushchair from Nik, but he held it out of her reach.

'I'm not going anywhere until I make sure my nephew is all right,' Nik said flatly. 'Now, stop wasting time and let's get Danny inside.'

Nik sat in the only armchair and watched Carrie tidying her flat with quick efficiency. She was still dressed in the tight-fitting exercise gear that must be what she wore for work. He felt his body stir with pure male appreciation as he admired her long-limbed yet curvaceous feminine shape.

There was no doubt that she was very well toned, and there

was something incredibly sexy about her swift and supple movements as she worked systematically around the single space that
seemed to serve as kitchen, dining area and living room.

The area was small, but as Carrie put Danny's things away
Nik saw that it was very well organised. The stylish design of
the place still spoke of Carrie's carefree days as a young single
woman, without any attachments or responsibilities, but the
child's things were fitted in neatly and looked as if they belonged.

Danny was sleeping in the bedroom. A dose of infant painkiller, a drink of warm milk and a long cuddle were all that it
had taken to send him off into what looked like a very peaceful
sleep. Carrie had spoken of the everyday ailments that babies
sometimes suffered from—quick to come and equally quick
to go. She'd seemed to know what she was talking about.

Nik had deliberately kept out of her way while she took care
of the baby, giving her the space and time she needed. He had
been impressed, and rather surprised by what he'd seen.

Since his first meeting with Carrie she'd seemed quite
jumpy, and full of nervous energy. He hadn't expected her to
be so calm and loving towards the child. Somehow he just
hadn't taken her for the warm, motherly type.

But recognising that Carrie did have some good points as
a carer did not change Nik's plan. This was not the way he
wanted his nephew to be brought up. No matter how well in-
tentioned Carrie was, she was on her own, and she still worked
full time. How could she possibly give the child what he, with
all the might of Kristallis Industries behind him, could give?

For instance, this flat was so small, and there was only one
bedroom. The cot took up most of the available floor space,
and there was no chance that an additional bed, even a child-
sized one, could be squeezed in next to Carrie's double bed
when Danny got older.

His blood stirred at the thought of Carrie's bed—or rather at the image of Carrie lying in it. It was a small double, but a double none the less, and that meant it was made for sharing. He flexed his fingers to prevent his hands clenching at the suddenly intolerable thought of Carrie sharing that bed with anyone.

'That'll do for now,' she said, startling him out of his thoughts as she paused for a moment with her hands resting on the curve of her hips. 'Coffee?'

'That would be perfect,' Nik replied smoothly, despite being caught deep in thought, and watched as she turned to fill the kettle with water.

God, but she was gorgeous! With her back still towards him, she stretched up into a high cupboard for the mugs. The simple action made her top ride up, separating from the black stretch pants that clung so alluringly to her shapely bottom and legs. Several inches of pale skin were suddenly revealed, and hot desire for her slammed into him, hard and unexpected.

Of course she was a good-looking woman. He was a red-blooded male and he'd been aware of that from the second he'd laid eyes on her. But suddenly he wanted her with a power that knocked the breath right out of him.

He remembered the way that pale skin had felt beneath his fingers, the way that supple body had melded so electrifyingly to his. He thought about yesterday's kiss, and instantly his heart was thumping powerfully in his chest.

He hadn't meant that kiss to be more than a simple distraction to enable him to replace the mobile phone in Darren's pocket. But once he'd been holding her lithe body in his arms, and she had moulded herself to him like a second skin, his animal desire had threatened to take over.

And if he didn't get himself under control soon, the urge to seize her and kiss her again might take over now.

But would that be such a bad thing? The rational part of his mind told him to avoid making a difficult situation more complicated. There was more at stake here than a passing fling with a gorgeous woman.

But Nik wasn't known for playing it safe. His instinct told him to pull her into his arms and kiss her senseless. She wouldn't object if he did. He'd seen her looking at him with those sexy green eyes, and felt the way she'd responded to him the previous day.

'It's only instant coffee, I'm afraid,' Carrie said, twisting round to look over her shoulder at him.

She sucked in a startled breath and stared at him warily. The raw intensity of his expression made her pulse start to race. He looked dangerous. He looked ready to spring up out of the chair and come towards her. What did he mean to do?

'Instant is fine.' Nik's eyes skimmed over her in a way that made her skin start to heat up alarmingly.

Carrie gripped the edge of the counter and turned back to the coffee, trying to ignore the mixture of anxiety and excitement that was suddenly coursing through her.

Why was he looking at her like that? A shiver ran down the length of her spine and she fought the urge to fidget. She knew she was being silly, overreacting like a teenager. But she still felt self-conscious. She could feel his eyes burning a trail over every part of her body.

'Do you take milk and sugar?' she asked, without looking round.

'No, thank you,' Nik replied.

She needed milk for her own coffee, and she stepped across the tiny kitchenette to the fridge, acutely conscious of his gaze following every movement she made.

It was ridiculous! She was a fitness instructor—used to people watching her body. Every day people focussed on the way she moved, and studied the precise alignment of her anatomy.

But as she bent down to pull a carton of milk out of the

fridge she was aware of her own body in a way she never had been before. The feel of his eyes on her made every action seem loaded with sexuality.

She knew he wasn't watching her with his attention on her posture or her muscle recruitment. She knew he was thinking about sex. Her whole body started to tremble.

She straightened up and turned back to the counter to pour a dash of milk into her mug, but her feverish body didn't co-operate with its usual precision. The carton slipped from her fingers and jolted against the counter, splashing milk over her hand and up her arm.

'Let me help,' Nik said, suddenly coming up behind her.

'It's all right,' Carrie said huskily, staring almost blankly at her milky hand. She was completely aware of Nik standing behind her. He was so close. If she reached for a paper towel she'd collide with his chest. His arms would close around her and they'd be kissing with all the fire of their first encounter.

He'd caught her unawares in Darren's study, and her own body had shocked her by responding so fervently. She knew it would be crazy to let it happen again, but an intoxicating yearning was building deep inside her. If he pulled her into his arms again she feared she'd be lost to reason.

'Let me see,' Nik said, taking a step closer and placing his hands gently on either side of her waist.

Carrie gasped and spun round to face him. As she turned his hands skimmed the circumference of her waist, tracing the narrow band of exposed skin. The sensation of his fingers brushing against her bare flesh set off a chain reaction of tremors quaking through her body, and she couldn't stop shaking. She knew he must be able to feel it because he was still touching her waist.

She was holding her milky hand out in front of her

gingerly, almost as if it was injured. Her palm was facing upwards with the fingers curled over, instinctively trying to contain the spilt liquid.

She swayed as Nik released his hold on her waist, but almost immediately his hands moved to support her again. He placed one gently under her forearm and the other he brought up carefully to cup her milky hand.

Carrie stared down at his bronze fingers curling round her. He was only holding her hand, but somehow it seemed too intimate. A knot of anticipation tightened deep within her and she licked her lips nervously.

'The paper towels are over there,' she said, hardly recognising the husky tones of her own voice.

'It's only a bit of milk,' he murmured. 'We don't need a towel.'

Slowly, ever so slowly, he lifted her hand up to his lips. She followed the movement with her eyes, hardly daring to think what he meant to do.

Suddenly she found herself looking across her palm, straight into his vibrant blue eyes. She could feel his hot breath on the skin of her hand and she swallowed hard.

His lips parted and, still ensnared by his burning gaze, she watched his tongue emerge to lick a drop of milk from a finger.

She sucked in a startled breath and thought vaguely of pulling her hand away. But before her whirling thoughts had a chance to settle he drew the finger slowly into his mouth.

Sensation flooded her, and the heat of his mouth seemed to radiate through her whole body. The sinuous feel of his tongue moving against her skin sent a tidal wave of longing crashing over her. Without realising what she was doing her own lips parted and a small sigh escaped.

Nik's eyes were fixed on her, registering her response, and immediately he pulled her closer. He released her finger and moved his open mouth over the skin of her palm, nibbling and teasing with his lips and tongue.

Carrie trembled. She didn't want Nik to know the effect he was having on her over-excited nerve-endings, but it was more than she could do to tug her hand out of her grasp. He pulled her closer and brought his lips to the sensitive skin on the inside of her wrist, flicking the tip of his tongue over the beating point of her pulse.

Her breathing quickened, echoing her racing heart, and she closed her eyes, trying to shut out the reaction that was rapidly taking over her whole body. But, instead of grounding her, the action left her completely cut off from any reality apart from Nikos Kristallis. She was only aware of how he was making her feel.

She wanted him to kiss her! She wanted to feel his hot mouth covering hers, feel his tongue moving against hers.

Her breath was coming in short sharp gasps, and although she tried, she just couldn't think about anything else. Suddenly she realised he had let go of her hand. Her eyes flew open, and she saw his face was only inches from her own.

The moment seemed frozen in time, yet only lasted a second. In slow motion she saw him lift his hands to cup her cheeks and incline his head slightly, ready to kiss her.

Then his mouth closed over hers, and her world exploded into a startling frenzy of desire.

Her lips were already parted as his mouth came down to kiss her, and their tongues were suddenly writhing together in an erotic dance. Her body trembled and she clung to his strong arms for support, overwhelmed by the blood singing wildly in her ears, the fervent uprising of excitement that threatened to completely engulf her.

She had one last coherent thought—she hadn't imagined the effect of his kiss yesterday. Then she closed her eyes and was lost as a rush of sensations powered through her bone-less body.

Her hands slipped up to his broad shoulders and she pressed herself close to him. His body felt so good, so hard and strong against hers. Her arms reached further round and she let her hands slide slowly across his strong back, feeling the heat of his body through the fabric of his shirt. She yearned to touch his naked skin, feel the play of his muscles beneath her questing fingertips.

All the time they kept on kissing, an ardent expression of their mutual desire, but she was getting increasingly breathless and her head was starting to spin. At last he pulled away from her lips, and she heard his breathing was as ragged as hers.

She opened her eyes to find herself staring into Nik's face, and suddenly plummeted back to the real world with a sickening jolt. Had she completely lost her mind? Why had she let Nik kiss her like that?

'What are you doing?' she gasped, hearing her voice rise with a hint of panic.

'Nothing you didn't like, that's for sure,' Nik replied, his cheeks darkening with strong emotion.

'I didn't like it.' Carrie took a step backwards and bumped hard into the kitchen counter. What was happening to her? She'd never let herself get so carried away before. She'd had no idea it was possible to be so utterly overcome by naked desire that she lost track of the world around her.

'You did like it,' Nik said, his blue eyes burning danger-ously. 'And you'd like it if I did it again. Don't lie to me, Carrie. I know what I felt—what we felt. The chemistry between us is incredibly powerful.'

'There's nothing between us,' Carrie said.

She stared at him, battling with conflicting thoughts and emotions. She didn't *want* there to be anything between them.

After all, Nik had barged into her life upsetting her and threatening to take Danny. But at the same time all she wanted to do was step back into his arms and let him kiss her again—let him do anything he wanted with her.

No man had ever had such a powerful physical effect on her. But it wasn't just physical. She'd had no idea that her body could respond with such raw sexual energy to a man, but her mind was overwhelmed, too. When she was in his arms all she could think about was how good it was, how incredible he was making her feel.

'A moment ago you wanted that just as much as I did,' Nik said.

'You're wrong,' Carrie muttered, leaning back against the counter and looking down at the floor. Oh, *why* had she let him kiss her?

'I'm not wrong.' He took a step closer and brushed his hand against her cheek.

An instant response shivered through her, but she straightened her shoulders and stared back at him defiantly, refusing to give in to her body's desires.

'You're crazy!' she said. 'Crazy and arrogant and…and I think it's time you left.'

'I'm not leaving yet,' Nik said flatly. 'We still have things to discuss.'

'I'm not talking about it any more,' Carrie said. 'It was a mistake and it will never happen again.'

'Why are you making such a big deal out of it?' Nik asked. 'I told you I'm not married, and neither are you. Do you have a boyfriend?' he added suddenly, looking at her sharply. 'Is that why you're so upset?'

'No!' she squeaked. 'But that's none of your business. Besides, I already told you—your marital status is of no interest to me.'

'You don't care whether your lovers are married?' he asked.

'Of course I do,' she said, thinking it would be a big mistake to let Nik know she was a virgin. 'But, since you are never going to be my lover, why should I care whether you are married or not?' She felt a dark prickle of excitement skitter through her body at the idea of being in bed with him, but she shied away from the thought in horror, appalled at her body's reaction.

'Don't be so sure about that. We both know what we felt just now,' he said. 'Besides, in the car you asked me straight out whether or not I was married. So I think I can be forgiven for assuming you were interested.'

'I just thought you must have children,' Carrie said quickly, thinking back to the awkward journey in the limousine. 'What with the car seat and the toys. That's all.'

'They were for Danny, of course.' Nik seemed surprised. 'How can you think I would come unprepared for him?'

'Prepared for what?' Carrie said in alarm. 'You went to Danny's nursery without my permission. You were planning to kidnap him! That's why you had those things!'

'You really have the most overactive imagination.' Nik's smile didn't reach his eyes.

'Then how come you were discussing who could take children out of the nursery with Mrs Plewman?' Carrie demanded in a stiff and quiet voice. 'She obviously told you an unauthorised person couldn't take a child—so you must have asked about it.'

'I already told you—I wanted to see where he was cared for,' Nik replied. 'I wanted to assess how safe he was there.'

'You *were* going to take him away!' Carrie gasped, convinced that had been Nik's intention all along. What if he really had driven Danny away in the limousine before she'd got there? Her chest felt so tight she could barely breathe, and her stomach churned in horror. 'You were going to abduct him and take him back to Greece!'

She'd been suspicious of Nikos Kristallis from the start, but he'd deliberately distracted and confused her with his magnetic sex appeal. Now the threat to Danny seemed all too real. Next to that, nothing else was important.

'I'll never let you have him!' she cried.

'I would not take the child without your knowledge,' Nik said, his glittering blue eyes darkening with anger. 'What kind of man do you take me for?'

'The kind of man who seduces someone just to get close to her baby!' Carrie declared.

'Danny is *not* your baby,' Nik said. 'And what happened between us had nothing to do with the child.'

'You have no more right to him than me.' Anger was rising up to take over from the sick horror that still swamped her at the thought of losing Danny. 'You're never going to take him from me!'

She planted her hands on her hips and matched his angry stare. He'd soon discover that she wasn't just going to step aside and give up a child she loved like her own.

'This is ridiculous! Why are you making such a drama out of it?' Nik asked. 'I give you my word that I will not abduct Danny and take him out of the country without your prior knowledge.'

'So you're going to tell me first, then take him?' Carrie asked. 'Great—that makes me feel a lot better!'

'No, I'm still working on the basis that we can behave like adults,' Nik said coldly. 'I assume we can work together to come to an agreement. A mutually beneficial arrangement that we both believe to be in the best interests of Danny.'

'You assume a lot!' Carrie said.

'That we can both behave like adults?' Nik asked, a hint of derision colouring his voice.

'That you can treat Danny like one of your business deals,' Carrie said. 'He's a human being, and we certainly won't be coming to any "mutually beneficial arrangements"—he's not a piece of property!'

CHAPTER FOUR

THE Mediterranean sun was hot on her back as Carrie sat beside the pool, waiting for her client, Elaine, to come out of the villa for her workout. She flipped through the glossy pages of a magazine, trying to keep her thoughts away from Nikos Kristallis. Even after three quiet days on the Spanish island of Menorca she was still on edge.

He couldn't get his hands on Danny here, she thought grimly. Or on her. That thought sent a shiver running down her spine, despite the heat of the sun.

Nik had been furious when he'd left her flat the other night, but when she'd asked him to leave for the second time he'd gone without further comment. Maybe he'd realised he was fighting a losing battle? Maybe he'd figured out that she'd never willingly give up Danny?

But surely that wouldn't stop a man like Nikos Kristallis? Wasn't he the sort who went to any lengths to get what he wanted? Carrie shivered again, wondering just how far Nik would go.

She was glad she'd brought Danny to Menorca. The trip was a work commitment that had been arranged for months, but as far as Carrie was concerned the timing was perfect. Although the situation with Nik was still unresolved, everything had suddenly become too intense. She needed some breathing room.

She'd considered letting Nik know about the trip, but in the end she'd decided against it. Why should she tell him? After all, he'd never shown any consideration for her. His constant assertions that Danny would be returning to Greece with him were really starting to worry her, and she was still horrified by what might have happened if she hadn't arrived at the nursery when she had. Despite the nursery's strict rules about who could collect children, she knew the extent of Nik's charm. There was no doubt he could be very persuasive.

'Here I am,' Elaine said, shrugging off her towelling robe as she hurried over to the table by the pool. 'Sorry to keep you waiting.'

Carrie smiled as her friend sat down. 'Yes, it's been really terrible waiting here for you, in the sunshine, reading a magazine…'

She glanced across to the shady spot under the trees where Elaine's nanny and her ten-year-old twin girls were playing with Danny. She could hear his giggles of delight and see how happy he was.

It was good to be in Menorca. They could both do with a pleasant change from their usual routine. It had been a long hard winter for Carrie and, although it was now early May, warmer weather had seemed reluctant to come to London that year. It was wonderful to escape for a while, and relaxing by a pool in the Spanish sunshine certainly beat pushing Danny's buggy round the dreary pigeon-pecked paths of her local park.

'Danny sounds like he's enjoying himself.' Elaine smiled, looking over at the children, too. 'The girls love having him here. If they get too much, you will tell me, won't you?'

'They've been fantastic,' Carrie said, thinking about the

way the girls had been doting on Danny, fussing over him every chance they got. 'You know how much I love being with him, but it's been wonderful to be able to relax and watch him playing with someone else.'

'You don't get much chance for that, do you?' Elaine asked. 'You work too hard, love. I know you have to make ends meet, but time flies by and you can never get this time back again.'

'I know,' Carrie said, suddenly feeling a twinge of guilt for sometimes wishing that life was less exhausting, and that Danny was older and easier to care for. Somehow it seemed as if all she did was work and look after the baby. Her social life had ground to a virtual halt

'Any juicy gossip?' Elaine asked, leaning over to peer at the magazine.

'I don't know,' Carrie said. 'I wasn't really reading properly.' Her eyes scanned the glossy celebrity photos, automatically looking for familiar faces.

Many of her clients were celebrities, and in the past she'd worked with even more famous people. After she'd started caring for Danny she'd had to drop a lot of her clients. The out-of-hours training sessions required by some of her regulars simply didn't fit in with her childcare arrangements. She'd felt bad about letting people down, but Danny had to come first.

She'd been lucky to find part-time work at a gym, and the rest of the time she devoted to clients like Elaine, who could train during the day, when Danny was at nursery.

'Ooh, look—it's Lulu and Darren,' Elaine said, tugging the magazine out of Carrie's grip. 'Isn't she one of your clients?'

'Yes,' Carrie said, unsettled by how quickly her thoughts had bypassed Lulu and settled on Nikos Kristallis kissing her in Darren's study.

'Maybe not any longer,' Elaine said. 'Look—it says Darren has thrown her out.'

'What?' Carrie gasped, pulling the magazine back and placing it on the table between them. Was that her fault? Had Lulu been right about how strongly Darren would react to the voicemail she'd left him? If only Nik hadn't interrupted her and she'd been able to get to Darren's phone in time.

'It says that she's been having an affair with another footballer!' Elaine said. 'Darren discovered them together last week at a party. There was a terrible scene, ending with him throwing her out!'

'How awful!' Carrie said, feeling torn apart on Lulu's behalf. But she couldn't help wondering exactly what had really been going on when Lulu had begged her to get the phone.

They both looked at the photographic evidence in front of them—a sequence of shots that apparently showed Darren and Lulu arguing, followed by pictures of Lulu leaving the house in tears.

There were lots of other photos of guests at the party. Some of them were celebrities, some were not well known, but all of them seemed happy to be photographed at the glitzy party. Carrie frowned, thinking how fickle the media was—happy to build you up when it suited them, and even happier to drag you down if it made a better story.

'Good grief—look at this!' Elaine hooted, pointing to a photo of a couple kissing. Their faces were pressed together, keeping their identities hidden, but there was no hiding the way the couple's bodies were intimately entwined in a position that was frankly sexual. The man's leg was pressed between the woman's thighs, pushing her skimpy red skirt up revealingly, and her back was arched so that her breasts were more than half exposed, and looked as if they were about to explode out of the dress altogether. 'That's positively indecent! Just what kind of party *was* it? Were you invited?' Elaine asked.

'What?' Carrie gasped, feeling her blood run cold as she looked at the photo.

Oh, God! It was a picture of Nik kissing her!

'Makes you wonder what goes on at these celebrity parties,' Elaine said. 'Some people have no shame. They'll do anything to get their photo in one of these magazines. Did you see all this going on?'

'No…no, I didn't stay at the party,' Carrie stammered. Her heart was pounding and she felt sick to her stomach. 'Ready for your workout?' she blurted, hoping Elaine wouldn't notice that she was shaking, and beads of perspiration had broken out on her clammy brow.

Elaine laughed and tossed the magazine back on the table.

'That's why I love you!' She smiled. 'You're so focussed. You never let me waste my workout time.'

'I think you'll enjoy the routine I've got planned,' Carrie said, inwardly wincing because she certainly wasn't focussed on Elaine at that moment. She continued speaking, trying to sound breezy and natural, when inside she felt like curling up and hiding. 'It's good to take advantage of the pool while we're here.'

'As long as it works,' Elaine said, patting her stomach and looking critically at her thighs. 'I haven't got long to fit into my outfit.'

'Your dress already looks great,' Carrie reminded her. 'And you're so much fitter. You know you've done brilliantly.' She was proud of how well Elaine had got back her fitness after an operation had prevented her from exercising for a while.

Carrie wasn't really concerned with how slim people were; she just wanted to help them achieve their fitness goals so that they could enjoy life to the full. In her work as a trainer she always put the emphasis on fitness over conforming to stereo-typed images of body size and shape. But she understood how important it was for Elaine to feel she looked good at her younger sister's wedding.

'Right—let's do this,' Elaine said, jumping into the pool.

Carrie switched on the portable CD-player, and immediately a funky dance beat filled the air.

'Okay, let's warm up,' she said, slipping into the water beside Elaine. She concentrated on the task at hand, hoping some hard work would burn off the stress adrenaline that was pumping round her body. As long as she didn't let herself think about that appalling photo she'd be all right.

In the past she'd always taught aqua-aerobics from the poolside, where she could keep her eye on a whole class. Earlier, when she'd been planning the session, she'd thought it would be fun to get in to the water and join in properly— now she was grateful for something that required a higher level of concentration from her.

She started off gently, taking Elaine through the unfamiliar moves, but before long both of them were thoroughly involved in the routine. Carrie almost felt disappointed as she came to the end of the cool-down and stretch section of the workout.

'That was really great,' Elaine said, climbing out of the pool and pushing her wet hair out of her eyes.

'I'm glad you enjoyed it. We'll do it again tomorrow,' Carrie said, pulling herself up out of the water. The tiles surrounding the pool felt deliciously hot under her wet feet as she walked across them to pick up a towel from the table.

She lifted the towel to dry her face, but as she closed her eyes behind the soft warm fabric a shiver suddenly darted down her spine.

Something was wrong. Elaine had started to speak, then suddenly gone quiet.

'What is it?' she asked, glancing quickly over to the children, who were still playing under the tree, and then back to Elaine.

'Who's that—talking to John?' she asked.

Carrie turned and followed Elaine's puzzled gaze across to the drive, where her husband John was talking to a tall, dark-haired man.

It was Nikos Kristallis.

'No! It can't be!' Carrie gasped. 'How did he find me here?'

'Who is it?' Elaine asked, looking at her sharply. 'Are you in some kind of trouble, Carrie?'

'It's… It's…' Carrie croaked, struggling to speak with a suddenly dry mouth. She swallowed hard and twisted the towel tightly in her shaking hands. She was rooted to the spot, hardly able to believe her eyes.

Nik stared at Carrie.

Satisfaction at finding her and the child mixed unpleasantly with a powerful rush of anger. Here she was, apparently having a whale of a time, frolicking around the pool in the sunshine, while he'd had to go to the trouble of ascertaining her whereabouts from her colleagues at the gym and then follow her to Spain. That wasn't how things worked in his world.

He turned and scanned the garden quickly. His eyes settled on Danny, who was sitting on a rug under a tree, with two older girls and a young woman who appeared to be looking after all three children. The girls were laughing and building a tower of blocks in front of him, and the young woman leant forward and adjusted the hat that had slipped down over Danny's eyes.

He seemed to be happy and well cared for, but that didn't excuse the fact that Carrie had taken him out of the country without informing him. He knew she was here to work, but as far as he was concerned that made no difference. The sharp pain from his fingernails digging into his palms told him he was clenching his fists too fiercely.

He turned his attention back to Carrie, and suddenly the

memory of their last evening together flashed unexpectedly through his mind. To make matters worse she appeared to have just stepped out of the pool. His body's hot response was out of his conscious control as he took in the sight of her, wet and glistening, dressed in a tiny clingy bikini.

'I need to speak to Miss Thomas.' He spoke briskly to the British gentleman who owned the villa, knowing his tone didn't leave room for debate.

Carrie was looking across the pool at him. He had seen her reel under the shock of seeing him, but now she was talking to the other woman and glancing across at the children.

He deliberately uncurled his fingers and forced himself to release some of the tension gripping his tightly coiled muscles. He took a few quick strides and suddenly he was standing right in front of her. Two hectic spots of colour danced on her pale cheeks, but she stood her ground and stared straight up into his face.

'What do you think you are doing here?' she demanded, planting her hands firmly on her hips and tossing her sleek black hair back from her face with a shower of droplets. Next to the wet blackness of her hair, her skin looked paler than ever, almost shimmering with the sheen of moisture that still clung to it. 'How did you find us?'

'Your colleagues at the gym were most helpful,' Nik said, thinking how it hadn't taken much to loosen their tongues.

'They had no right to tell you,' she said through gritted teeth. 'And you have no right to barge your way into my client's house. I'm working,' she added.

'I have every right to be concerned over the welfare of my nephew,' Nik replied, keeping his eyes firmly on her face and not giving in to the desire to run his gaze down over her exquisite body.

'Well, as you can see, he's perfectly fine.' Carrie folded her arms across her chest. 'Not that it's any of your business. I look after him and I decide what's best for him.'

She glared up at him, determined to keep her cool, but it wasn't easy when she was standing there in nothing but a bikini. He was so tall that standing in her bare feet, she had to tip her head right back to look at him properly.

It was hot beside the pool, but the heat of the Spanish sun was insignificant compared to the burn of his gaze. She couldn't help fidgeting slightly, curling her toes against the hot tiles, then dropping her arms down to her sides before promptly folding them again.

'You may be Danny's guardian at the moment,' Nik said. 'But pull any more stunts like that and you'll soon find out who you're up against.'

'You think I'll just roll over and let you do whatever you want?' Carrie gasped. 'Danny means everything to me. Do you think I'd care if I found myself up against you?'

As soon as the words had left her mouth she realised how they sounded. Or maybe it was only to her own ears. But she couldn't stop her gaze sliding down and taking in the broad expanse of his chest. She knew exactly what it felt like to be pressed up against him, and she couldn't stop her body responding to the memory.

She knew all about 'muscle memory', where muscle groups seemed to have their own recall of a sequence of movements in dance or exercise. But she'd never heard of 'body memory'— which was surely what she was experiencing now. Her whole being seemed to be buzzing with the memory of their bodies pressed together and bending as one as he pushed her back over Darren's desk. If she wasn't careful she'd find her body stepping forward of its own volition and melding provocatively to his.

Nik narrowed his eyes and a smile flashed across his tanned face.

'In fact, I can see you definitely *would* care to come up against me—again.' He tilted his head and let his deep blue eyes sweep suggestively down her exposed body.

The touch of his gaze was almost as potent as the touch of his hands. It felt as if he'd run his fingertips across her skin, leaving a sizzling trail of sensation in their wake and starting a slow-burning fire deep within her body.

Carrie sucked in a shaky breath and hugged her arms defensively over her breasts. But she knew she hadn't stopped him noticing the sudden tightening of her nipples beneath the wet bikini. And she couldn't hide the hot flush which was creeping across her bare skin.

She simply wasn't used to her body reacting like this, and she didn't know how to handle it. She'd never realised that she could experience such powerful and confusing sexual feelings.

'Should I ask this man to leave?' Elaine asked crisply. She had been standing politely to one side, to give Carrie some space, but now she stepped closer and handed Carrie her own towelling robe. 'John and I certainly won't put up with anyone bothering you while you are in our home.'

Carrie turned away slightly and gratefully pulled the robe on. She belted it tightly and made herself look back up into Nik's face with a confidence she didn't really feel. She wanted Elaine and her husband to make him leave, but she knew they had to sort this out now. Besides, somehow she doubted whether *anyone* could actually make Nik leave if he wasn't ready to.

'Miss Thomas and I have not finished our discussion yet,' Nik said arrogantly. 'And we would appreciate a little privacy, if that would be convenient for you.'

'Just hold on a minute—' Elaine started to bluster.

'It's all right.' Carrie spoke to her friend, making her voice sound bright and confident. 'There are some issues that Mr Kristallis and I really do need to clarify.'

'I'll be just inside with John,' Elaine said. 'Call me if you need anything.' She gave Nik a hard stare, then turned reluctantly and headed across the lawn to gather up the children and the nanny.

Carrie looked back at Nik. He was watching Elaine pick up Danny and carry him away into the villa. The intense expression on his face made her shudder.

He continued to stare into the dark interior of the villa for a few moments longer, then suddenly his piercing blue gaze turned back to her. But she was ready for him and spoke before he had a chance.

'Let's get this straight,' Carrie said firmly. 'You have no right to storm in here and demand explanations from me. I am under no obligation to report my plans to you.'

'No, you're not. At least *not yet*,' Nik added. 'But what about common decency?'

'Decency!' Carrie gasped. 'That's rich, coming from you—the man who forcibly kisses total strangers just because he feels like it, and who barges uninvited into other people's homes whenever it suits him!'

'And you're so perfect?' Nik asked. 'By taking Danny out of the country you've done exactly what you accused *me* of planning.'

'I haven't abducted him,' Carrie said. 'It's up to me to decide where I want to take him.'

'And to do whatever you want without any regard for other people?' Nik demanded. 'I gave my word never to take Danny anywhere without your knowledge. And even as I made that promise you were planning to get on a plane with him a few hours later!'

'That's different—' Carrie started.

'Perhaps you would be so good as to tell me your plans now?' Nik interrupted coldly, as if whatever reasons and explanations she was about to offer were completely immaterial to him. 'How long are you staying in Menorca and where are you intending to go when you leave here?'

'I shall be staying here with Elaine's family until Friday,' Carrie said quietly. Suddenly there didn't seem to be any point in making things more difficult between them. 'And then I shall return to my flat in London and carry on like normal.'

'All right,' Nik said. 'You may stay here and honour your work agreement. But that is on the strict understanding that you will not agree to any similar undertakings in the future.'

'My work is none of your business. I don't need your permission,' Carrie said in exasperation. 'I keep telling you that.'

'But where you and Danny go and who you see *is* my concern,' Nik said. 'I keep telling *you* that, but since you seem to have difficulty accepting it, I shall be leaving my assistant here in Menorca while I return to London to complete some business.'

'You're going to leave someone here to keep an eye on me?' Carrie gasped. 'Who do you think you are?'

'You know who I am. I've never tried to conceal my identity from you or mislead you about my intentions,' Nik said. 'You, on the other hand, don't have such a shining record. Let's not forget what you were up to when we first met.'

'I wasn't up to anything,' Carrie said, feeling her cheeks blaze. A rush of images spiralled horribly through her mind—Nik catching her red-handed in Darren's study, Nik kissing her, the appalling photograph of them kissing that she'd just seen in the magazine.

She gritted her teeth and stared up at him, refusing to let her thoughts continue down that path. She flicked her damp fringe out of her eyes and tried to look confident and unperturbed by his comments.

'I know what you told me,' Nik said. 'Surely you don't think it's wise to get involved with that sort of thing?'

'I was doing a favour for Lulu,' Carrie said. 'What's wrong with helping a friend out?'

'Considering what Lulu was up to under her husband's roof, with one of his best friends, I'd say the answer to that question hinges on your attitude to adultery,' Nik said.

'You don't know the whole story,' Carrie said defensively, actually wishing that she'd known what was going on before she'd agreed to do Lulu's dirty work. But there was no way she'd admit that to Nik. 'There are always two sides to these things.'

'Maybe more than two sides,' Nik said. 'After all, you were in Darren's study. Perhaps you were there for a secret liaison with him.'

'Now you're being ridiculous,' Carrie said. 'Anyway, I thought he was your friend. That's not exactly very loyal of you.'

'Acquaintance rather than friend,' Nik replied. 'But I do know what he's like, and it's fair to say he can give Lulu a run for her money. And, as I said, it was Darren's study and you were certainly dressed to impress.'

'If that's the case, why didn't he mind when *you* kissed me?' Carrie threw at him.

'He recognised he'd met his match?' Nik asked.

'He was virtually cheering you on!' Carrie snapped. 'It was humiliating!'

'Is that how you found it?' Nik asked.

'Of course it was humiliating to see my photo in that trashy magazine!' The awful full-colour image that she'd seen on those glossy pages flashed nauseatingly through her mind.

'Oh, you saw that?' Nik drawled, as if seeing himself portrayed like that meant nothing to him.

'You had no right to put me in that position.' She suddenly felt her cheeks blaze as she remembered exactly how she'd felt as he pushed her back over the desk, his leg pressed intimately between her thighs while he kissed her.

'I got the impression that position turned you on.' The corner of his expressive mouth twitched, as if he found her embarrassment amusing. 'I thought you found our little encounter quite stimulating.'

'That's not what I meant.' Carrie glared at him, despite the overwhelming urge to turn away and hide her blazing cheeks. 'You had no right to drag me into your sordid little celebrity scandals!'

'As I recall, it was your ill-advised foray into Darren's study that led to our little clinch in the first place,' Nik said dryly. 'I hope you've learned your lesson and now realise it's not very sensible to get involved with that kind of thing.'

'Don't you dare patronise me!' Carrie gasped. 'If I choose to do a favour for one of my friends, it's none of your business!'

'While you are caring for my nephew, everything you do is my business,' Nik said.

'And what about you?' Carrie demanded. 'It was your outrageous behaviour that resulted in that appalling photo. Who knows what other unsuitable activities you might have been indulging in?'

'I do not need to make an account of myself to you,' Nik said.

'But you think I need to explain myself to you?' Her eyes flew over him with irritation, standing there so cool and perfect in his immaculate designer suit. He oozed wealth and power, from the top of his arrogant head to the leather soles of his handmade Italian shoes. 'You've had life so easy. You have no idea what it's like for the rest of us—having to question our actions, worrying whether we made the right decisions.'

'Of course I question my actions,' Nik said coldly. 'Having money doesn't make you immune to difficult decisions.'

'No, but it makes it a whole lot easier.'

'I have to live with bad choices I've made, just like everybody else.' Nik pushed his fingers roughly through his dark brown hair.

'Poor little rich boy,' Carrie said. 'Do you expect me to feel sorry for you?'

'Okay, let's just stop it!' He took off his jacket and slung it over his shoulder. 'I didn't come here to argue with you. I only wanted to ascertain where you and Danny were.'

Carrie stared up at Nik, suddenly breathing very quickly. His outburst had startled her, making her stomach feel fluttery.

He was studying her again. His full lips were pressed together and his brows were drawn down, casting his blue eyes into deep shadow. The muscles in his face were tense, pulling his bronzed skin taut across his high cheekbones and around the strong, darkly stubbled curve of his jaw line.

'What time is your flight back to London?' he asked, suddenly businesslike.

'Late Friday morning,' Carrie said warily. 'We are all flying back together.'

'My assistant, Spiro, will stay with you until then, to make sure you and Danny are all right,' Nik said. 'Unfortunately I have to return to London to sort out some business.'

'He can't stay here,' Carrie said. 'This isn't my place, you know. I won't have you ruin Elaine's family holiday by leaving someone here to…to stalk me!'

'Believe me, it's not my first choice,' Nik said. 'But it will have to do. If you try to evade Spiro I shall return at once and place both you and Danny under my care, in a location where you can be closely supervised.'

'Are you threatening to abduct us?' Carrie gasped. It was a nasty reminder that dealing with Nikos Kristallis was dangerous. There was so much at stake.

'Still so over-dramatic,' Nik said calmly. 'Just don't do

anything stupid in the next few days. I have to try and salvage something from a business deal that collapsed when you pulled your disappearing act.'

'Why are you doing this? You don't care about Danny at all!' Carrie burst out. 'He's just a big inconvenience because you had to choose between him and clinching a business deal!'

'Don't talk about Danny as if he means no more to me than some kind of acquisition,' he said. 'Even though you seem unable to accept it, he is my nephew and I care about him.'

'Then why did it take you six months after your brother died to come and find his orphaned baby boy?' Carrie demanded. 'You just thought it would be more convenient to wait until a business trip brought you to London anyway.'

'I didn't know he existed,' Nik grated. 'Until very recently I didn't know he existed.'

A flash of raw emotion passed across his face for a split second and Carrie stared at him in surprise. Was he telling the truth? She wanted to know how it was possible that he hadn't known about Danny, but then a movement from the villa caught her eye. Elaine was approaching, with a bottle of mineral water and two glasses.

'I thought you might need some refreshment,' she called out as she came towards them.

'Thank you for your concern.' Nik turned to speak to Elaine. 'But it's not necessary. I was just about to leave.'

'But…' Carrie was suddenly lost for words, still wondering about what Nik had just said.

'I'll meet your plane when you return to London next week,' Nik said, turning on his heel and striding away towards the wrought-iron gate at the villa driveway.

'You look like you need a long cool drink,' Elaine said, pouring water into a glass.

'Thank you,' Carrie said, with only part of her attention on her friend. She was watching the tall dark figure of Nikos Kristallis as he climbed into the back of his black limousine.

He had frightened her with his announcement that he'd only learned about Danny's existence recently. The fact that he hadn't waited six months to seek out his nephew but instead had come virtually straight away was unnerving. It seemed to make it even more certain he really *did* plan to take Danny from her.

She was glad that he had gone, but a nasty cold feeling of dread crept over her.

CHAPTER FIVE

THE appalling heat in the underground car park was the final straw as Carrie searched in every corner of her bag for the keys to the hire car. She'd looked and looked, even emptied the contents of the bag out onto the dusty bonnet of the car—but the keys simply weren't there.

Danny had come down with a case of chickenpox, and was screaming agonisingly in her ear. Her head was spinning and tears pricked behind her eyes as she desperately tried to think what to do next.

Only one thing was clear. She had to get Danny out of that car park quickly, before his fever got dangerously high. The poor little thing was burning up, and if she couldn't find the keys to the hire car she'd have to find some other way to get him somewhere more comfortable, where she could try to cool him down.

She started stuffing things back into her shoulder bag with one hand while she held Danny in her other arm, trying not to rub his irritated skin or press him too close to her hot and sticky body. It wasn't an easy task, especially with her eyes blurring with unshed tears and a lump of anxiety constricting her throat. What if she couldn't cope? What if she couldn't take care of Danny properly, make him well again?

The nightmare had started that morning, when they'd got ready to leave for the airport. Danny had seemed grizzly, and then one of Elaine's girls had noticed the small red spots. Carrie hadn't known what they were, but Elaine had recognised them immediately. Chickenpox.

The airline doctor had agreed with Elaine and refused to let Danny fly home.

At first Carrie had felt quite calm. She'd just have to stay in Elaine's villa with Danny until he wasn't infectious. It would be fine. She knew where everything was. There was food in the freezer and there was a small grocery shop a few metres along the road.

Elaine had been more worried, fretting and saying she'd stay behind, too. But she had her sister's wedding, and Carrie knew how much that meant to her. Then John had offered to stay instead, but Carrie had insisted she'd be all right on her own with Danny. After all, she looked after him on her own at home.

She'd done such a good job sounding confident and convincing for Elaine and her family that she had more or less convinced herself, too. Luckily she had her driving licence with her, and John had just had time to hire a car for her before their flight left. And then they'd had to go, leaving her alone with Danny and the keys of the villa.

He had seemed all right while she drove away from the airport, and she'd been proud of herself for staying so calm. When she'd caught sight of Nik's assistant's car in her rearview mirror she had smiled grimly and thought to herself that she wasn't exactly alone anyway. No doubt he'd already called Nik to let him know she wasn't on the plane.

She'd decided to stop in town to buy some infant painkiller, just in case she needed more and they didn't stock it in the village shop near the villa. That was when everything had started going badly.

Danny had become increasingly distressed, and by the time she'd got back to the stifling underground car park he'd been far too hot and screaming at the top of his lungs.

For the first time that week Nik's assistant had disappeared, so she couldn't even ask him for help. She was feeling so desperate she would have asked almost anyone around. But the car park was deserted.

Oh, why had she assured everyone she'd be all right on her own? She didn't feel all right, and Danny certainly didn't look or sound all right.

She grabbed a tube of suncream just as it slid off the car bonnet and tried to get it into her bag, but the strap of her bag had started to slip off her shoulder. A moment later her bag and all its contents were scattered on the grimy concrete floor of the car park.

She stared at the mess in utter dismay. It was too much! But somehow she had to get through it because Danny needed her.

'It's all right, Danny,' she said, in a falsely high and squeaky voice. Her words didn't reassure him or stop him crying at the top of his lungs.

'It'll be okay,' she said again. But as she spoke she heard her own voice crack. She pressed her quivering lips together and squeezed her eyes shut to stop the tears from falling.

She couldn't bear to hear Danny in such distress. She had to keep it together and think of what to do next.

She squatted down next to the car and started picking up the essentials, like her purse, Danny's water bottle and the keys to the villa. The suncream and rest of the stuff would just have to roll around under the car until she could deal with it.

The most important thing was to get Danny out into the fresh air, give him some infant painkiller and get him to drink something. Then she would think what to do after that.

'What the hell are you doing?' a deep voice behind her grated. 'Why didn't you get on the plane with the others?'

She recognised the voice immediately. It was Nikos Kristallis.

'Oh, thank God you're here!' Carrie said, standing up and turning round to face him. Despite the harsh tone of his voice, she had never been more grateful to see anyone. She felt tears of relief swim in her eyes, and she spoke quickly before she really started crying. 'Danny's sick, and they wouldn't let me take him on the plane. He's burning up, and I need to get him out of this sweltering car park, but I've lost the car keys.'

'What's wrong with him?' Nik asked sharply, reaching out to take the child.

'Chickenpox,' Carrie replied, letting him take Danny without objecting. She was too hot and sticky, and she knew it was making the fevered baby feel even worse. 'The first thing we have to do is get him out of here and cool him down.'

'Come on,' Nik barked, instantly striding towards the exit. He shot a series of comments in Greek to his assistant. 'Leave your things. Spiro will bring them.'

Carrie hurried along beside Nik, keeping close enough so that Danny could easily see her. But he wasn't really looking. He'd stopped howling and his head was lolling against Nik's shoulder. She didn't think that was a good sign.

'We'll go to a hotel and call a doctor,' Nik said. 'I saw a hotel just down here.'

Carrie was almost running to keep up with his long stride, and it seemed as if only moments passed before they were marching into the foyer of the hotel. Carrie was watching Danny so closely that she hardly registered Nik's rapid conversation with the receptionist, but they were quickly shown into a large hotel room.

'The doctor will be here very soon,' Nik said, turning to

face Carrie. She was looking at Danny and biting her lip anxiously. 'What do we do now, before he gets here?'

She stared up at him with wide green eyes, and for a moment she seemed almost surprised that he had asked her what to do. Then her gaze flicked straight back to Danny.

'Try to cool him down,' she said quickly. 'Get him to sip some water, and it's time to give him another dose of painkiller.'

Nik laid Danny carefully on the bed and sat beside him to take off his shorts and T-shirt. He stared at him in shock, appalled at the sight of his little body covered with red spots.

It was unacceptable! No Kristallis baby should have to endure this. No nephew of his should be dragged around hot and crowded public places while he was sick. God knows what Carrie would have done if he hadn't arrived when he had.

'Oh, no!' He heard Carrie's sharp intake of breath. 'There's twice as many spots as this morning.'

'He doesn't feel so hot as when I first took him.' Nik lifted Danny and placed him awkwardly on his knee. 'It's air-conditioned in here. Maybe that's helping.'

'I'm sure it is,' Carrie said, kneeling down beside them and tearing open a sachet of painkiller. She started to squeeze out the syrupy liquid onto a spoon. 'It's very cool in here. That car park was unbearably hot.'

'Yes,' Nik said dourly. He didn't need reminding. Danny should never have been in a place like that in his condition.

'Here you go.' Carrie popped a spoonful of pink medicine into Danny's mouth. 'That will make you feel better. Now, a few sips of water to wash it down, that's a good boy.'

Carrie sat back on her heels and studied Danny thoughtfully. She was starting to feel less anxious.

'He seems a bit better,' she said after a moment. She reached out and took him carefully from Nik. 'I mean, of course he's still sick, but his temperature is not dangerously high any more, and he's looking at me now and trying to smile a bit. I was so frightened when he wouldn't respond.'

She hugged him gently, pressing her face against his curls, and looked at Nik, who was still sitting on the bed.

'Thank you,' she said. 'Thanks for helping us out like this.'

'There's no need for thanks.' Nik stood up abruptly. 'Danny is my nephew. Naturally I would do whatever I can for him.'

'Well, you turning up when you did certainly made things easier,' Carrie said. She was grateful for his help, but at that moment an uncomfortable wariness crept over her. Would he find a way to use this against her? Would he say it proved she was an unsuitable guardian for Danny? 'Of course we would have managed on our own,' she added. 'I just needed to get Danny somewhere cooler.'

She looked up at him, standing over her, and a shiver prickled between her shoulderblades. Suddenly he seemed incredibly tall, incredibly powerful. He was looking down at her with an unnerving intensity that made her wish she wasn't kneeling on the floor.

'Where's that doctor?' he asked impatiently. He glanced at his watch and strode across the room. 'He should be here by now.'

'He'll be here in a minute,' Carrie said, to reassure herself as much as anything. She stood up and moved away to the other side of the room. Waiting with Nik was making her feel jittery. Thankfully at that moment there was a knock on the door, announcing the arrival of the doctor.

Carrie hesitated by the door that linked the two hotel rooms and looked at Nik. He was sitting at a little table, working on his laptop computer. He hadn't noticed her come in, and that gave her a moment just to look at him.

The jacket of his suit and his silk tie were lying on the bed, and he had rolled up the sleeves of his white shirt and undone the top button while he worked. He was completely absorbed in his task, and his tanned fingers were flying over the computer keys with a speed that surprised her.

He looked so rigidly focussed that he reminded Carrie of an athlete, centering himself before a crucial event. For a second she envied him. He always seemed so sure of himself, so certain of what he wanted and what to do next.

She had been so relieved to see him when he'd turned up in the car park, and was truly grateful for the decisive way he had taken control, bringing them to the hotel and calling the doctor. However, things did not seem so straightforward now. He'd been very helpful, but there had been an edge to his manner that made her feel anxious. What would he expect in return?

She glanced around the hotel room and frowned. Nik had the only chair, which meant she'd have to sit on the bed or stand about looking awkward. Or tiptoe back into the other hotel room, where Danny had finally fallen asleep.

She hadn't realised at first that Nik had booked adjoining hotel rooms for them. She didn't know what he intended, but all she wanted to do was return to the villa and wait until she could take Danny home.

The doctor had confirmed the previous diagnosis of chickenpox and told her what to expect over the next few days and what to do to keep Danny comfortable. It shouldn't be too long until he wasn't infectious and would be allowed to fly.

Suddenly Nik turned round and caught her watching him. A smile flashed across his face so quickly she thought she might have imagined it, and then she felt his brilliant blue eyes ensnare her. She was fixed in his gaze, and it almost felt as if he was tugging her towards him.

She'd been studying him a moment ago, but now the tables

were turned and she was the one being watched. She felt her pulse leap and her senses move onto red alert.

'Danny's sleeping now,' she said quickly, unsettled by how breathless her voice sounded. 'I'll leave this door open a fraction so we'll be sure to hear if he wakes up.'

'Come and sit down,' Nik said quietly, careful not to disturb the sleeping child. 'We need to discuss our immediate plans.'

Carrie walked across the room, feeling absurdly self-conscious, and sat down. She didn't want to sit on his bed, but she wasn't about to make a big deal out of it.

'Spiro brought your things up while you were with Danny,' Nik said, closing his laptop and lifting his chair round so he could look at her straight on.

'Thank you,' Carrie said, glancing behind her to the pile of things Nik had indicated. 'Oh, my suitcase and everything! That was locked in the boot.'

'Spiro found the keys on the ground under the car. They must have fallen out of your bag,' Nik explained, lifting one hand to unconsciously massage the back of his neck.

'That's a relief,' Carrie said, watching him roll his head from side to side. She knew he was acting instinctively, to relieve the stiffness in his neck, but the incredible sensuality of the movement suddenly caught her deep down inside.

Her heart started to race, her legs felt shaky and her mouth ran dry. It was an unfamiliar feeling for her, but even so she recognised it for what it was. Pure sexual attraction.

Nikos Kristallis was the sexiest man she had ever seen—and it wasn't just his gorgeous good looks. The way he moved his body affected her in the most alarming way. The sinuous roll of his head from one powerful shoulder to the other. The way he flexed his muscles and tilted his head as he lifted his hand to rub his neck.

Her fingers itched to touch him—touch him in a way she

had never touched any man before. She wanted to slide her hands down over the contours of his hard muscled chest, feel the heat of his body, lean forward and press her face against his skin and inhale his masculine scent.

'That's all taken care of now,' Nik said.

'I'm sorry?' Carrie said, shaking her head sharply to clear her mind. She shook her hair back from her face and focussed on Nik carefully, concentrating on what he was saying. She didn't like realising she had lost the thread of the conversation while her mind ran away with such blatantly sensual thoughts about Nik. 'What's taken care of?'

'Spiro is returning the hire-car to the airport. You won't be needing it any more.'

'He can't take it back. I *do* still need it!' Carrie exclaimed, suddenly completely back in the moment. 'I need it to drive to the villa, and to get about until Danny's given the all-clear to travel.'

'That's what I wanted to talk to you about,' Nik said. 'I can take you home.'

'Danny can't fly,' Carrie said.

'He can't fly on a public flight while he's infectious,' Nik agreed. 'Luckily, I have my own plane.'

'Your own plane!' Carrie echoed Nik's words in surprise. Just how rich *was* Nikos Kristallis? 'Is that how you got to Menorca so quickly when I didn't get on the flight home?'

'No, I simply jumped on the first flight to Menorca out of London Gatwick,' Nik said. 'It was quicker than getting to my own plane, which was at another airport. I don't usually use major airports—too many people, too many delays.'

'Oh,' Carrie said, not quite sure how to respond to the information that Nik was obviously even wealthier than she had thought. 'Sorry you had to rough it by travelling with the public.' She looked down and her eyes settled on the tie Nik had left lying on the bed. Without thinking she picked it up and smoothed her fingers along it. 'Anyway, if you left your plane at another airport, how can you offer us a ride home?'

'It will be here later this evening,' Nik said, letting his gaze drop to her lap, where she was unconsciously tracing the pattern on his tie as it lay across her thighs. 'Until then you can rest in the hotel.'

'It's not necessary.' Carrie slid the silky fabric of his tie between her hands. It was tempting to accept his offer, but she didn't want to be even more indebted to him than she already was. He was still dangerous to her, and she mustn't let herself forget it just because he had helped her out of a difficult situation. 'Danny and I will be quite all right staying at Elaine's villa.'

'I think it's best if I take you home,' Nik replied, his eyes still fixed on her hands. God, she was turning him on! Watching the sensual movements of her fingers playing with his tie was pure erotic torture. If he didn't feel those sexy hands on his body soon he was going to explode. 'I can't stay here. I have work I must do.'

'I didn't ask you to stay here!' Something in her voice made him look up, and the expression on her flushed face told him she had finally realised what she'd been doing with his tie. And that she'd seen him watching her sensual actions.

Her heated cheeks revealed that she knew how it was affecting him, and as that fact sank in her own body was responding in kind. She wanted him as much as he wanted her.

She tossed her head in a gesture of denial and stood up jerkily, dropping the tie as if it had suddenly burnt her fingers.

'I'm grateful you came when you did, but now we'll be perfectly all right on our own.' She folded her arms defensively, but lifted her gaze to meet his.

'There's no point taking chances.' Nik stood up and moved a step closer to her. He wanted to feel her hands on his body, caressing him the way she had caressed his tie. 'I'm going to take you home tonight.'

'So when you said that we needed to discuss *our* plans, you meant you needed to tell me *your* plan?' Carrie placed her hands firmly on her hips. She stood her ground and looked him squarely in the eye.

Another bolt of desire ripped through Nik as he looked down at her. She seemed unaware that her defiant posture was thrusting her breasts towards him in a way that was almost impossible to resist.

'If you have another idea that is better, I'll listen to it before I make a decision.' Nik narrowed his eyes and tilted his head slightly as he studied her.

There was an enticing naïveté about her sexuality that experienced women didn't normally have. Oh, he was quite sure she'd had her share of lovers—how could such a sensual creature not have experienced physical love?—but there was still a freshness about her actions that drew him.

'Don't think for a moment I'm going to leave you alone in a strange country with no one to watch over you, though,' he added.

Carrie swallowed, and unconsciously drew her lower lip into her mouth as if she was struggling to maintain eye contact with him. Her teeth pressed gently into her lip as she concentrated, but her gaze slipped down and he guessed she was staring at the vee of bronzed skin at the open neck of his white shirt.

She was looking at him as if he was irresistible, and that turned him on like nothing else before. He was used to women falling all over him, but there was something different about this. She wanted him, but she was fighting it. It was the biggest aphrodisiac he had ever experienced.

Nik lifted his brows slightly as he continued to look at her. 'Do you have another course of action to suggest?'

'What?' Carrie asked, blinking as if to clear her mind. She looked up at him, clearly trying to appear as cool and collected as she could. 'I'm sorry. I lost my train of thought. I was miles away for a moment.'

'Not that far away,' Nik spoke quietly, deliberately letting his voice drop to a deep, seductive tone. 'You were right here all the time— with me.' A buzz of anticipated conquest ran through him. Despite her resistance she was going to be so easy to seduce.

'I'm tired,' Carrie said. She tossed her fringe back and tried to stare him down, even though she could feel herself blushing furiously. She had to brazen it out. She couldn't let him know just how much he was affecting her. 'It's been a long day, but I'm still capable of making my own decisions.'

'What do you suggest?' Nik asked.

Carrie thought hard for a moment.

'Take us home,' she said. 'But don't get any funny ideas about it. I'm only doing what is best for Danny.'

'Funny ideas?' Nik echoed, his Greek accent more pronounced as his gaze skimmed sensually across her body. 'What could be funny about taking you home?'

'You know what I mean,' Carrie insisted, ignoring the wave of heat that moved through her as his eyes swept over her. 'Nothing is going to happen between us.'

'Even though you want it to?' Nik asked huskily.

Suddenly he seemed too close. He was an overwhelming physical presence that sent the prickle of goosebumps shivering over her skin and a ripple of undeniable sensual desire washing through her.

She had never felt such a strong attraction to any man before, but she knew she must not let herself be distracted by it. She was tired, she hadn't eaten all day, and she was grateful for his help. But she must never forget the threat Nik posed to her and Danny's happiness

'I *don't* want anything to happen between us.' Carrie folded her arms tightly over her breasts.

Talking about it suddenly filled her with a rush of excitement that sent her pulse soaring and started a quiver of desire deep inside her. Who was she kidding? She couldn't deny the overwhelming need she felt for him—but she knew it made her too vulnerable.

Nikos Kristallis already exerted too much power over her life. Too much was at stake to let him have any more advantages. Her attraction for him frightened her.

She remembered with vivid clarity how her incredible desire for him had almost left her at his mercy that evening in her flat. What if she lost control again?

'I've seen the way you look at me,' Nik said huskily. 'You want me to make love to you.'

'No, I don't!' Normally she appreciated plain-talking people who said what they meant—but Nik's sudden directness left her gasping for breath with her cheeks blazing.

'Are you protected?' Nik continued, as if she hadn't spoken and wasn't going scarlet with embarrassment.

'What?' Carrie's mind was spinning. Why was he talking about protection? She certainly needed something to keep her safe from him—at that moment he seemed just like a deadly predator moving in for the kill.

'For when we make love—are you protected?' he pressed again.

'Oh!' Carrie felt her cheeks heat up even more as she finally realised he was talking about contraception. For a moment she couldn't believe he'd asked her such a thing— how had things gone this far? 'Yes—I mean no! Look, there's no need to worry about that,' she said. She was never going to let things go that far!

'That's good,' Nik said softly, moving even closer. 'I would be honoured to make love to you. But I understand why you're holding back.'

'You arrogant beast!' Carrie gasped, unsuccessfully trying to flick her suddenly damp fringe back from her face and willing her cheeks to cool down. 'I know you must be used to women queuing up to climb into your bed, but some of us are immune to your charms!'

'So you admit I have charms?' Nik's blue eyes glittered with laughter.

'No, I don't,' Carrie said crossly. She pushed back the strands of hair that clung damply to her forehead with a jerky movement, upset that he was making fun of her.

'I'm sorry,' Nik said. 'But you know everything will be all right. After all, we both want the same thing.'

'No, I don't know anything of the sort!' Carrie said. 'We hardly know each other, so stop acting like you know me or what I want!'

'You're scared of yourself,' Nik said quietly. 'You don't want to give in to your feelings for me in case it complicates things.'

'I'm not scared!' Carrie snapped, horrified by how well he had read her. 'And I certainly don't have feelings for you!'

'I think there's more between us than mere sex.' Nik lifted his hand and laid his palm gently against her cheek.

'There isn't… We haven't…' Carrie stammered, unconsciously leaning her blazing cheek into the soothing coolness of his palm.

'The physical expression of our desire is burning between us,' Nik said, slipping his hand round to cup the back of her head and taking a step closer to her. 'We can both feel it surrounding us, pressing us together, buzzing through our bodies like electricity.'

'I can't—' Carrie started, then forgot what she was going

to say as Nik leant forward, his lips hovering only a fraction above hers.

His words were spinning through her mind and body as if they were tangible things. She really could feel some kind of energy surrounding her, pressing her closer to Nik.

She was breathing rapidly. Her heart was beating fast. She knew he was going to kiss her. She wanted him to kiss her.

She stared at him with wide eyes. Their faces were so close that he was slipping out of focus and she could feel his breath hot on her skin. His hand behind her head held her firm and she let her eyelids slide down. Then she was only aware of the moment. She was poised, waiting for his lips to find hers.

'I want you to touch me,' Nik murmured against her mouth, the teasing movement of his lips almost, but not quite, a kiss.

Carrie's eyes flew open, but he was still so close that she couldn't see him clearly.

'I want you to touch me,' he repeated, and his lips moved against hers again.

'No—' Carrie started to protest, but as she spoke her lips brushed tantalisingly against his, making hot liquid desire suddenly pool deep inside her. She wanted to press closer and kiss him properly.

'Touch me—like you were touching my tie,' Nik murmured, every syllable an exquisite, delicate torture. She felt the strong suppleness of his lips, and could imagine the flick of his tongue as he formed the words.

'I don't...' She paused and took a breath. She tried to pull back but he was still holding her head. She closed her eyes— it was impossible to think clearly. All she wanted to do was open her mouth and run her tongue along Nik's lip. All she ought to do was pull away from him decisively—show him that she didn't want this—but she felt too weak to move.

'I know you want me to kiss you, and I will.' His words

sent sparks of electricity zinging through her body. 'But first you have to touch me.'

'No.' She wouldn't play his games. It would be playing with fire.

'I know why you don't want to.' His mouth brushed hers. 'You're afraid—afraid that once you start you won't be able to stop. You'll want to tear my clothes off and push me down on the bed. You'll want to press your face against my skin, taste me, lick me, kiss me.'

Carrie made an involuntary sound deep in her throat and screwed her eyes even tighter shut. She'd never ever even thought about licking a man before, but now Nik had said it all she could think about was how his skin would feel under her tongue. What would it taste like? Would it turn him on?

Oh, God! What was happening to her? She didn't want to turn him on! She wanted him to leave her alone.

'Maybe I'm mistaken,' Nik murmured as he moved his free hand and started sliding it down her bare arm. Carrie held her breath. He'd done the same thing in Darren's study right before he kissed her.

He caught her hand in his, lifted it up to his chest, then moved back slightly to allow a little space. She stifled a moan of protest as his lips left hers, but then became aware of the feel of his hot skin beneath her fingertips. He'd undone one more button of his shirt and slipped her hand inside.

Carrie stood stiffly, staring in alarm at her own hand that was resting just inside the open collar of Nik's white shirt. She wanted to snatch it away, but at the same time she wanted to glide it across his chest. She couldn't do either, because Nik was still holding her wrist, keeping her hand firmly in place.

'If I'm mistaken, and you're not burning to touch me, then it should be no problem to demonstrate just how indifferent you are,' Nik said. 'But I can feel the chemistry buzzing between us. I know what you want to do.'

'I don't…' Carrie paused, trying to steady her quavering voice. 'I don't know what you mean. What is this supposed to prove?'

'When you were stroking my tie, running your fingers backwards and forwards along it, you were thinking of me, thinking of touching me,' Nik purred.

'I wasn't.' Carrie swallowed, trying desperately to keep her hand still, but she could feel the heat of his skin beneath her fingertips and she wanted to feel more.

'No? Well, maybe it was just me, fantasising about the feel of your hands on my body.' Nik looked at her through long dark lashes. 'Maybe I was projecting my desire onto you.'

Carrie bit her lip, unable to speak. His words seemed too much to take in, but her body was already responding to them. The thought that he'd fantasised about her hands touching him sent her pulse soaring and make her tingle deep inside.

'Show me how you feel,' Nik said. 'Run your hand across my body just like you smoothed it along the silky length of my tie. I want to look into your eyes as you touch me.'

'No, I'm not going to play your games,' Carrie said. She avoided meeting his gaze, but the sight of her hand inside his shirt was almost as unsettling.

'I said you were afraid.' Nik smiled. 'Afraid of the attraction between us.'

'I'm not afraid,' Carrie protested. 'And I don't need to prove anything to you.'

'Indulge me.' Nik's voice was a low, seductive purr that rolled right through her.

She held her breath and looked at him, wondering what to do. His gorgeous face was so close to hers and he was giving her every ounce of his attention. For an absurd moment she felt as if she was the only woman in the world.

He wanted her to touch him, and she wanted the same thing. Alarm bells were ringing in her mind but she ignored them. She could do this. Satisfy her desire to touch him, then pull away and pretend she was indifferent. He had challenged her, and if she didn't rise to the challenge he'd never let it drop.

'All right.' She looked him boldly in the eye as a surge of courage fuelled by excitement stormed through her. 'I'll show you I'm immune to your charms. But are you sure your ego will be able to take it when I don't swoon at your feet?'

Nik said nothing, but dipped his head and focussed on her from beneath half-closed lids. He released his hold on her wrist, leaving her free to withdraw her hand if she wanted.

She didn't want to. She just couldn't resist the temptation to make the most of this opportunity.

She could feel the ridge of his collarbone, and she slipped her hand along it up to his powerful shoulder. Then she traced her fingertips gently back to the hollow at the base of his throat. His skin felt silky and smooth and she wanted to feel more.

She laid her palm flat and started to slide it downwards across the top part of his pectoral muscle. She'd seen his well-developed pecs through his shirt, and she had an overwhelming desire to feel his muscle swell against her hand and find his nipple with her fingertips.

Suddenly her hand was stuck, her wrist blocked by his next button, which was still tightly fastened.

'I said I wanted to look in your eyes.' Nik's deep voice startled her, then he cupped his hand under her chin and tilted her head towards him. 'Feel free to rip the buttons off, if the desire takes you that way,' he added, his eyes glittering.

'There's no need,' she replied, dismayed by how breathless her voice sounded. She looked up into his deep blue eyes, determined to brazen it out. She had to convince him of her indifference.

She lifted her free hand and undid the next button, and then the next one for good measure.

Her hand glided lower, and the well-defined bulge of his muscle felt as amazing against her palm as she had anticipated. Her fingertips brushed over the taut skin on his chest, and then she found his nipple.

A sudden release of hot melting desire turned her insides to liquid. Her fingers had itched to touch him, but she'd never guessed that stroking him would be as arousing as the feel of his hands touching her.

'Look at me.' Nik's voice rumbled through her, vibrating deep into her feminine centre.

She gasped, startled again by the strength of her desire, by her body's physical response to his voice.

'I said, look at me.' His voice resonated through her again, making her blood sing.

She blinked in confusion, realising that her eyes had slipped out of focus.

She pulled herself together and stared at Nik, overwhelmed by how powerfully she was reacting. His eyes, dark and sultry with obvious sexual need, were fixed on hers. She wondered vaguely if her own eyes were giving her away, but soon her mind was full of her own desire.

She let her fingertips circle his nipple, brushing against it with delicate teasing touches. She felt it stiffen against the pads of her fingers and she rubbed it lightly, then pinched it between her finger and thumb.

All the time she was looking into Nik's eyes. The deep blue colour was growing darker and his lids were sinking lower. There was no doubt as to how he was responding to her caresses, and that thought made her desire sharper still.

If offer card is missing write to: The Harlequin Reader Service, 3010 Walden Ave., P.O. Box 1867, Buffalo, NY 14240-1867

NO POSTAGE
NECESSARY
IF MAILED
IN THE
UNITED STATES

BUSINESS REPLY MAIL
FIRST-CLASS MAIL   PERMIT NO. 717-003   BUFFALO, NY

POSTAGE WILL BE PAID BY ADDRESSEE

**HARLEQUIN READER SERVICE
3010 WALDEN AVE
PO BOX 1867
BUFFALO NY 14240-9952**

Do You Have the LUCKY KEY?

PLAY THE Lucky Key Game

and you can get

FREE BOOKS and FREE GIFTS!

Scratch the gold areas with a coin. Then check below to see the books and gifts you can get!

YES! I have scratched off the gold areas. Please send me the 2 FREE BOOKS and 2 FREE GIFTS for which I qualify. I understand I am under no obligation to purchase any books, as explained on the back of this card.

304 HDL EL44   104 HDL ELUT

FIRST NAME

LAST NAME

ADDRESS

APT.#

CITY

STATE/PROV.

ZIP/POSTAL CODE

www.eHarlequin.com

2 free books plus 2 free gifts

1 free book

2 free books

Try Again!

Offer limited to one per household and not valid to current Harlequin Presents® subscribers.
Your Privacy – Harlequin Books is committed to protecting your privacy. Our Privacy Policy is available online at www.eHarlequin.com or upon request from the Harlequin Reader Service. From time to time we make our lists of customers available to reputable firms who may have a product or service of interest to you. If you would prefer us not to share your name and address, please check here. ☐

'You said you didn't want to touch me,' Nik said, his voice impossibly deep.

'I didn't want to,' Carrie replied, amazed at how steady she managed to keep her voice. 'I was proving a point, like you wanted me to.'

'I think we've proved the point,' Nik said huskily.

'No,' Carrie protested. Then her voice dried up as Nik took a step closer, trapping her hand between them.

'Now I'm going to kiss you,' he said, leaning close so that once again his lips were brushing hers.

'No,' Carrie gasped, but her body was already humming with desire.

'I asked you to touch me,' Nik murmured against her lips. 'And in exchange I said I'd kiss you.'

'It wasn't like that,' Carrie said. 'You're making it sound like…like…'

'Like we're both consenting adults free to express our desires, free to tell each other what we want?' Nik asked. 'Don't worry. I like that in a lover. I want to know your fantasies. I want to know how to satisfy you.'

Carrie's mind was spinning and her body was buzzing with overpowering desire for Nik. But her response to him was suddenly frightening her. She'd thought she could play Nik at his own game, but now she knew she'd been mistaken. He was a confident, sexually experienced man. She'd never even had a serious boyfriend.

She pulled away suddenly, taking a step backwards so that she was pressed up against the door frame.

A knock at the door right beside her head made her jump, and she jerked her hand free of his shirt, popping off several buttons in the process.

'I ordered Room Service,' Nik said, glancing down at his torn shirt. He didn't seem in the least moved by his damaged shirt, or surprised by the sudden intrusion, but he made no move to open the door. 'I thought you probably hadn't eaten today.'

'Room Service?' Carrie echoed in confusion, struggling to pull her thoughts together.

'You should eat,' Nik said, suddenly stepping round her and opening the hotel room door. 'I've got work to do before we leave.'

Carrie blinked as a trolley was wheeled in. She leant against the safety of the wall and took a moment to recover herself, while Nik signed for the food and tipped the waiter.

But she knew it would take more than a moment recover herself. Her legs felt weak and her heart was still racing. Her lips still tingled where he had brushed his against them, and an incredible yearning was building up inside her. She wanted him to kiss her. And that was not all she wanted.

'I didn't know what you'd like,' Nik said, apparently completely oblivious to the way she was feeling as he indicated the trolley that was loaded with a startling amount of food. 'Eat what you want, and if I have time after I finish this work I'll grab a bite as well.'

He'd never meant to kiss her, she realised with a jolt. The thought sent a ghastly weight slamming down to the pit of her stomach. He'd known that Room Service was coming all along—known that they'd soon be interrupted. He'd just been playing with her.

She was still reeling from what had happened between them, yet apparently he had totally switched off. The desire she'd thought she'd seen in his eyes and heard in his voice had completely evaporated.

'I'm not hungry,' she said, feeling the words stick in her dry throat as she moved towards the doorway into the other hotel room. 'I'm going to check on Danny. Then I'll try to get a bit of rest myself.'

Even though she hadn't eaten all day, the thought of food suddenly made her feel sick, and getting away from Nik was the most important thing.

'Before you go—' Nik called her back. 'I'll be needing your passports.'

'What?' Carrie turned and stared at him in confusion.

'To make arrangements,' Nik explained, sitting down at his laptop and opening it up.

'Oh.' Carrie paused. She'd almost forgotten that she'd agreed to Nik taking her and Danny home. 'But I thought we were going in your private plane. We don't need tickets for that.'

'We're still travelling from one country to another.' He didn't look up from his laptop, and the tone in his voice suggested he was stating something that was blindingly obvious.

'Oh,' Carrie muttered again, going through to get her bag. It wasn't *her* fault she wasn't used to travelling by private jet. He didn't have to treat her like an idiot.

'Here you are.'

He still didn't look up, so she placed the passports on the table next to the laptop and slipped quietly back into Danny's room.

CHAPTER SIX

CARRIE woke up with a start and realised straight away that the plane had landed.

'It's time to go,' Nik said. 'I've already carried Danny out to the car.'

'I'm coming,' she said, getting groggily to her feet. She didn't remember falling asleep, and even now it was a struggle to wake up properly. 'Sorry—I'm a bit wobbly.'

'You've had a difficult day,' Nik said. 'It's not surprising you're exhausted.'

'I suppose so,' Carrie said. She peered out of the plane window and frowned. It was dark, and she couldn't see much, but it didn't look at all familiar.

'This doesn't look like Gatwick,' she said.

'It's not,' Nik said. He picked up Carrie's hand luggage and moved towards the exit.

'Where have you brought us?' Carrie asked. He had already told her he used small airports. This must be one of them.

'Corfu,' Nik said. 'Come. You'll want to be with Danny, in case he wakes up.'

'What?' Carrie gasped in surprise. She couldn't have heard him properly. Even someone as arrogant and controlling as Nik couldn't have brought her to a foreign country without her permission. 'Corfu?' she repeated in sheer disbelief. 'You said you'd take us home!'

'I didn't say your home,' Nik shrugged. 'This is my home, and it is a much more suitable place for Danny to recover.'

'It wasn't your choice!' Carrie cried, hardly able to believe what she was hearing. A terrible day had suddenly got a whole lot worse. 'You deceived me. You've brought us here against my will!'

'It's for the best,' Nik said. 'There's no need for you to be cooped up in that dismal little flat. Obviously you will be more comfortable in my home. You can relax and Danny can have the best care to aid his recovery.'

'I want you to take me home to London,' Carrie said coldly, digging in her heels and refusing to move. 'It's what we agreed, and you know it.'

'Whatever for?' Nik sounded genuinely surprised. 'What is so important in London?'

'My job, Danny's nursery, our home!' Carrie's voice rose as she spoke.

'Danny can't go to nursery while he's sick,' Nik said. 'So you can't work. And don't expect me to believe you'd rather be stuck in that tiny flat than taking it easy in my home.'

'I'm not discussing this with you. It's my decision, not yours,' Carrie said firmly, wishing she felt as confident as her voice sounded. 'I'm getting Danny and taking him home, *to London*, right now.'

'How are you planning to do that?' Nik asked, lifting his dark brows superciliously. 'You'll have no more chance of getting him on a flight here than you did in Menorca. What's more, I'm not going to risk my nephew's well-being by leaving him in your care when you're obviously not thinking straight.'

'I wasn't thinking straight when I trusted you to take us home,' Carrie snapped. Tears were pricking behind her eyes but she blinked furiously, determined not to let him see how upset and helpless she felt.

Nik paused at the exit and looked back at her, his broad shoulders virtually blocking the view of the airport behind him.

'By now Danny is safely in a car that is ready to take him to my home,' he said. 'Whether you join us is up to you, but Danny is coming home with me tonight.'

He turned calmly and started down the steps to the tarmac below.

Carrie dashed after him, her heart pounding as she burst through the doorway into the warm night air.

'Wait!' she shouted, stumbling precariously on the top step and grabbing the metal rail to keep her balance. 'You can't do this.'

'Of course I can.' Nik turned and looked up and her, his expression utterly implacable. 'It's already done.'

'But you lied to me!' Carrie cried. 'This is kidnapping!'

Nik studied her for a moment, not even bothering to defend himself, and then he pulled something out of his jacket pocket.

'Here's your passport,' he said, tossing it up to her. She caught it instinctively. He also put her bag down on the step beside him, so she could pick it up as she passed. 'You can do as you wish. Danny stays with me.'

Oh, God! Her stomach plummeted as she stared at the passport in her hand. Nik still had Danny's!

'Wait!' she shouted again, clanking down the steps behind him. 'Give Danny's passport to me right now,' she demanded, snatching up her bag from the step as she passed.

'I'm going home,' Nik said over his shoulder. 'You may do as you wish.'

Carrie stared in dismay as he strode across the tarmac away from her. Her stomach was churning and she felt horribly sick. She couldn't believe this was happening, but she knew if she didn't follow him he'd soon be driving Danny away into the Greek night without her.

She did the only thing she could. Gripping her shoulder bag tightly, she started to run after him.

Carrie stared out of the window as the limousine made its way swiftly through the one-way system of Corfu Town. It was late at night, but there were still a surprising amount of people about.

She'd never been to Corfu before, but she knew it was a busy tourist spot, popular with the British. If only she could get Danny away from Nikos Kristallis, surely there would be people she could ask for help?

She glanced sideways at Nik. He was leaning forward, watching the sleeping baby with an unsettling intensity.

'I need to stop here in town,' Carrie said suddenly, knocking on the window that separated them from the driver. 'Could you ask your driver to pull over?'

'Whatever you need will be provided at my home,' Nik said, picking up the internal telephone to communicate with the driver. 'There's no need to stop.'

Carrie gritted her teeth and looked through the glass to see the man talking to Nik on the telephone link. She had expected him to slide open the glass that separated them. But she knew without Nik's support she didn't have much chance of persuading his driver to stop for her.

'I need to pick up some things for Danny and for me. I didn't expect to be away from home for so long,' Carrie tried again.

'Don't think about doing something foolish.' Nik turned to look at her. 'I have Danny's passport and a copy of his birth certificate. He is my nephew and my family is well known here. No one will help you take the child out of Corfu without my permission.'

Carrie bit her lip and went back to staring out of the window. They were driving through the countryside now. It was dark, but she could see that the road was winding its way through dense olive groves. She tried to concentrate on remembering the route, so that she could retrace it on her own if she got the opportunity. But all she could think about was how foolish she'd been.

She'd played right into Nik's hands. It would have been very hard for him to take Danny out of England without her consent, but she had done it for him.

Of course she hadn't known Danny would come down with chickenpox, but Nik had been all too quick to turn that to his advantage. She should never have accepted his offer to take her home. And she should definitely not have handed over Danny's passport.

'My home is the other side of this mountain,' Nik said. 'It is quite isolated, so please don't try stumbling about outside. I don't want you falling down a rocky path.'

'Really?' Carrie asked nastily. 'If I broke my neck falling off a mountain, surely that would solve all your problems?'

'Not if you kill yourself on my property,' Nik said coldly. 'I should also warn you that the very best modern security system protects the perimeter of my land. You won't be able to leave with Danny.'

'You mean I'm your prisoner.' Carrie glared at him.

'Not at all. You are quite free to leave any time you choose,' Nik replied.

'No one will try to stop me?' Carrie asked suspiciously.

'My staff will have orders to take you anywhere you want to go,' Nik said. 'But you will not leave with Danny.'

Carrie tossed her hair back and turned to the window. She

should be paying attention to her surroundings. The limousine was climbing into the mountains, sliding slowly round an alarming series of hairpin bends.

Surely this couldn't be the same road they had been driving along a minute ago? That one had been narrow and windy enough, but nothing like this hair-raising track. They must have turned off the main road, but she had missed the junction.

The limousine went slowly and carefully, but Carrie couldn't help feeling jittery. She only hoped they didn't meet another car coming the other way.

She glanced at Nik, but he appeared completely oblivious to the fact that the limousine seemed to be clinging precariously to the side of a mountain. Instead he was studying Danny intently, a slight frown creasing his strong forehead.

'He's been asleep a long time,' he said. 'Is that normal?'

Carrie blinked in surprise, caught off kilter by Nik's sudden question.

'I think so,' she said. 'After all, it is his usual bedtime.'

'But he slept a lot of the afternoon, and he hasn't had anything to eat or drink.' Nik leant forward and brushed a gentle hand over the sleeping child's brow.

'No doubt he'll make up for it later.'

Nik was acting like a concerned father, Carrie thought with a worrying stab of anxiety. It was good that he was genuinely concerned about Danny, but it was making her feel uneasy.

'Should we wake him?' Nik turned to look at her.

It was dark inside the limousine, but Carrie could tell his sharp eyes were scrutinising her. Instinct told her that it wouldn't be a good idea to wake Danny, but now Nik and his questions were making her feel worried.

'How long till we arrive at your place?' she asked.

'Only a few minutes now,' Nik said.

'Let's wait and see if he wakes up naturally when we move him,' Carrie said. 'If he doesn't, we can wake him and give him a drink, see if he's hungry.'

'I'll call ahead and have some food prepared.' Nik pulled out his mobile phone. 'What does he eat?'

'It's all right. I have a jar of food in my bag,' Carrie said.

'A *jar*?' Nik repeated incredulously, the disapproval plain in his deep voice. 'Obviously we have very different standards, but don't think for a minute you will feed my nephew mass-prepared convenience food in my home.'

'It's a good brand,' Carrie said, feeling slightly defensive. She cooked fresh food for Danny at weekends if she could, but she did feel a little guilty over giving him shop-bought meals at other times. 'It's organic,' she added, 'and, most importantly, now that he's feeling ill, it's what he's used to, and I know he likes it.'

At that moment Danny made a little murmuring cry. Both pairs of adult eyes were instantly fixed on the infant, who was finally stirring from his long sleep.

Nik stared at Danny in alarm. Was it normal for a baby to howl quite so loudly? He didn't know, but in the confined space of the limousine the noise was almost unbearable.

Fortunately it was only a matter of moments before they arrived at the villa. He led the way swiftly through the building to the suite of rooms that had been prepared for them. A cot had been brought in and placed close to a large bed that Carrie could use.

'Shall I call the housekeeper to help you?' he asked, speaking loudly to be heard over the incredible racket Danny was still making. 'Her English is not good, but she has many grandchildren so she will know what to do. Is there anything else you need?'

'I'm used to managing on my own,' Carrie said, perching

on a chair and offering Danny his beaker of water. 'But perhaps someone could warm a little milk?'

'Of course,' Nik said. He took a step backwards, then turned and walked out of the room, issuing orders to his assistant.

He sat down in the adjoining room and opened his laptop. He would use the time to catch up on some work, and also keep an eye on the proceedings in the next room.

It was a long night. After his milk Danny settled down a bit, but not for more than a few minutes. Carrie walked around the room holding him in her arms. She tried laying him down in his cot while playing a gentle melody from a music box. She even tried rocking him in his buggy. The night wore on, but whatever Carrie tried Danny just wouldn't sleep. She was beginning to look dead on her feet, and Nik was starting to think he should call the housekeeper to help.

Then, eventually, Danny's head drooped onto Carrie's shoulder and he was quiet. Nik watched her ease herself carefully down onto the bed, and miraculously Danny didn't stir.

He saw Carrie's eyelids slide down. She was so exhausted that she was asleep in a moment. Danny was sleeping too, nestled snugly against her, although he had slipped down and was supported by the bed, with his little tousled head resting in the crook of her arm.

Nik watched her sleep. He couldn't help but admire her beauty as he looked at her jet-black hair spread out on the white pillow behind her head, her long black lashes making a delicate arc on the pale skin of her cheek.

The grey light of dawn was just forming outside, and it had been a long, tiring night. But it wasn't quite over yet, and when a murmuring whimper caught Nik's ear his gaze instantly flicked back to the baby.

Danny had started to stir again. In a moment he would be fully awake and howling at the top of his lungs.

Nik knew what he had to do. He crossed quickly and silently to the bed where they were lying. In her sleep Carrie had relaxed her hold, and it was easy to slip Danny gently away from her.

CHAPTER SEVEN

The sun was streaming in through a chink in the curtains when Carrie woke up. She jerked into a sitting position and gazed groggily around the unfamiliar room. Her mind was foggy and for a moment she couldn't remember where she was.

Then the previous day's events came flooding back—Danny coming down with chickenpox, Nik bringing them to Corfu without her knowledge and against her wishes, and then, finally, the long night spent comforting Danny.

Suddenly she realised Danny was gone. She stumbled to her feet and looked wildly round the room, but he was not on the bed or in the cot.

Nik had taken him! He was probably halfway to Athens, or wherever else he had a house, by now.

Maybe not, she thought, forcing herself not to panic. She had to keep her head until she found out what had happened. She hurried to the door, but despite her best efforts to stay calm, her heart was in her mouth as she opened it and burst through into the adjoining room.

She stopped in her tracks and stared.

The room seemed to be full of people gathered round the sofa, where Danny lay on his changing mat, having his nappy changed by an older Greek woman. Carrie guessed she must be Nik's housekeeper, Irene, because she seemed to know what she was doing and was keeping Danny's attention with a lively stream of chatter.

'You're awake,' Nik said, glancing at her briefly before turning his attention back to the sofa, where Irene was slipping Danny's legs smoothly into his sleepsuit and fastening the poppers with a deft hand. 'I'll send for some food.'

He issued a series of orders and a younger woman who had been hovering near the door hurried away. Irene scooped Danny up, then turned and passed him carefully to Carrie before leaving as well.

Carrie's heart-rate had started to ease once she'd seen Danny was safe, but nothing beat having him back in her arms again, and she cuddled him tightly. He was no longer flushed and sweaty, as he'd been last night. He seemed much more settled as he curled up comfortably against her shoulder.

'You frightened me, taking him like that,' Carrie said. 'What happened? Why didn't you wake me?'

'You'd barely had any sleep at all when he woke up,' Nik said.

'I would have managed,' Carrie said, pressing her face into Danny's curly hair. 'That's what looking after a sick child is like. You can get by on hardly any sleep if your baby needs you.'

'It's not necessary for you to risk my nephew's well-being by running yourself into the ground,' Nik replied. 'You're not on your own any more.'

Carrie stared at him crossly. She couldn't stand his arrogant attitude, but she didn't want to start arguing with him right over the top of Danny's head.

'Nevertheless, I want your word that you won't take him from me again when I'm sleeping,' she insisted.

'It was an exceptional circumstance,' Nik said with a shrug. 'Hopefully the child won't keep you up all night again any time soon.'

His glib response was infuriating, but Carrie bit her tongue because at that moment the young woman returned, carrying a tray loaded with food and drink.

'Here is your breakfast,' Nik said, gesturing to the young woman to take the food outside onto the balcony. 'Danny has eaten and taken some milk. Now, if you'll excuse me, there are things I must attend to.'

With that he walked out of the room, leaving her alone with Danny. Carrie stared after him in irritation, then turned and stepped through the open door onto a long balcony that seemed to wrap itself around that end of the villa. The young Greek woman was waiting by the table, which was laid with a generous breakfast.

'Would you like some coffee? Or anything else to eat?' she asked politely.

'No, no, there's more than enough here,' Carrie said, realising just how thirsty she was as her eyes settled on the frosty jug of juice.

'Would you like me to hold the baby while you eat?' the young woman offered.

'No, thank you.' Carrie smiled. 'He can sit on my lap. We'll be fine on our own. Thank you,' she said again, relieved when she took the hint and left them alone.

Carrie sat down at the table and looked at the array of food, feeling slightly overwhelmed. She'd hardly eaten yesterday, and although she was absolutely ravenous she didn't know where to start.

She poured herself a glass of fresh juice and lifted it to drink. She paused, the glass forgotten halfway to her lips, and stared with wide eyes at the incredible view from the balcony.

Nik had said his house was in the mountains, but Carrie had never imagined the sheer breathtaking beauty of its setting. Verdant wooded slopes, shimmering with the iridescent silver-green leaves of olive trees, dropped dramatically down to a glittering turquoise sea. The tall thin spikes of cypress trees punctuated the landscape, and the rusty brown exposed rock of the mountain across from Nik's house provided a stunning backdrop.

It was a perfect Mediterranean day, and a more beautiful setting would be hard to picture. Carrie stood up and carried the now sleeping Danny nearer to the edge of the balcony, so she could look at the view properly.

For the last seven years she'd lived in London, where the view from her window was the rather dull sight of the flats across the road from her. Before that, at her aunt and uncle's house, she'd had a small side room with a view of their neighbours' garage roof. She couldn't even begin to imagine what it must be like to live somewhere so beautiful.

She took a long drink of the cool juice and looked out at the clear blue sky. The ground fell away sharply beneath the villa, and the tops of the cypress trees undulating gently in the breeze close to the balcony made her feel as if she was in a tree house, suspended above the awe-inspiring terrain.

Awakened by the orange juice, her stomach growled, and Carrie turned back to the table. Her mouth watered at the sight of the succulent fresh figs with their rosy centres, and thick white Greek yoghurt drizzled with amber honey. She sat down and started tucking in to a hearty breakfast, making up for the meals she'd missed the day before.

Carrie took a last bite of a very sweet sticky pastry, covered with chopped nuts and a delicately flavoured orange syrup, then leant back in her chair with a sigh.

The balcony was a very pleasant place to sit, and after all the stress of the previous day it felt good to hold the sleeping baby in her arms, but she really ought to transfer him to his cot.

She stood up, carried Danny inside, and laid him in the

travel cot that had been set up in the small living room adjacent to the bedroom. She stood back and held her breath, hoping he wouldn't wake. Then she tiptoed quietly through the bedroom into the *en-suite* bathroom, removed the clothes she'd been wearing for more than twenty-four hours and took a quick shower.

A few minutes later she was just slipping into a clean dress when Nik's voice coming from behind nearly made her jump out of her skin.

'He's asleep,' he said. 'Good. We need to talk.'

She spun round to see Nik standing in the doorway, watching her with an unnerving intensity in his deep blue eyes. He reminded her of a predator, waiting for its moment to strike, and she felt her heart start to beat faster.

'Don't you ever knock?' she asked hotly, quickly buttoning up the front of her dress. She was acutely conscious of how his dark gaze had settled on her exposed cleavage and a wave of heat washed through her body. Suddenly her stomach was fluttering, and she was catapulted straight back to the way he'd made her feel in the hotel room in Menorca. A minute earlier and he'd have caught her in her underwear—or even wearing nothing at all.

'I'm sorry if I startled you.' Nik sounded far from apologetic as he strode right into the bedroom and shut the door. 'I approached quietly, so as not to disturb the child. We should talk without distraction.'

Carrie's eyes flicked to the closed bedroom door and a sense of danger coiled through her. She wanted to suggest they move to a different room, but she didn't want Nik to realise that she was feeling intimidated by him.

She looked back at him, noticing for the first time that he'd taken the opportunity to freshen up too—his hair was still wet from the shower and he had changed his clothes. The short-sleeved ivory shirt and dark trousers were less formal than his usual sleek designer suits, but they didn't make him seem any less imposing.

'I'm here to discuss Danny's future,' Nik said. 'There are decisions that must be made immediately.'

'Good.' Carrie straightened her shoulders and looked him squarely in the eye. 'I appreciate you getting right to the point, but before we continue there is something I need to make absolutely plain.'

'What is that?' He watched her through narrowed eyes, looking irritated that she had something to say that delayed his personal agenda.

'You are not to do anything without my agreement,' Carrie said. 'Bringing us to Corfu without my permission was unacceptable. I won't be naïve enough to fall for anything like that again.'

'That's behind us now,' Nik said, not giving her the assurance she was after. 'What's already happened is no longer relevant. We're here now, with decisions to make that will affect all our futures.'

'It's relevant to *me*!' Carrie exclaimed. She wasn't ready to let that incident drop yet—not until he'd acknowledged he was in the wrong. 'You blatantly deceived me! You took—'

'You keep saying Danny is important to you,' Nik interrupted. 'If that's the case I suggest you stop delaying our discussion about his future.' The menace in his voice warned Carrie that he was not going to lose sight of his goal easily. Well, neither was she.

'I will never give Danny up.' She spoke clearly and plainly, hoping it was the best way to make him understand.

'Nor will I,' Nik said. 'That is why I have come to offer you a compromise.'

'A compromise?' Carrie repeated. If he was going to

suggest they shared custody she wouldn't agree. She might, at a pinch, agree to visitation rights. But she'd never ever give Danny up, even part time. It wasn't just that she'd promised Sophie and Leonidas, she had grown to love Danny too much to ever let him go—especially to a controlling, duplicitous man like Nikos Kristallis.

'You will marry me,' Nik said. 'And like any other married couple we will share his upbringing.'

Carrie stared at him in shock.

Had she heard him properly? Maybe the sleepless nights were finally catching up with her. That must be it, because he couldn't possibly, in all seriousness, have said she was to marry him.

'What did you say?' she asked, her voice scratching her suddenly dry throat.

'We will be married,' Nik said.

'Are you crazy?' she gasped, staring at him in astonishment.

'Not at all,' he replied. 'Marriage is the only solution if you wish to retain any contact with Danny.'

'I'm not marrying you,' Carrie said, finally realising he really meant it—although she still couldn't believe she was actually having this conversation. 'I've never heard anything so ridiculous in my life. I don't even *like* you!'

'A marriage of convenience is the only compromise I'm prepared to offer you,' Nik said coldly. 'And take note that it is a one-time only offer. You must agree to it now or you will lose Danny for ever.'

'How can you call it a compromise?' Carrie asked, hearing her voice rise with appalled disbelief. 'Unless you mean I am to compromise all my values and beliefs by marrying someone I despise!'

'*I* am making the compromise.' Nik's voice cut like steel through the air. 'Marry me and you will still be part of

Danny's life. If you refuse I'll have you escorted off my property today and you will never see him again.'

'You can't do that!' Carrie cried.

'I can do anything I want.' There was a dangerous edge to his words. 'Now, what is your answer?'

'I'll never give up Danny!' Carrie said, horrified to feel tears prick behind her eyes. She blinked them away, refusing to show any weakness in front of Nik. He was detestable, coming to her and making such an unbelievable demand.

'I'll take that as your agreement.' Nik turned to leave. 'I will start the arrangements for our marriage straight away.'

'No!' Carrie flew across the room and seized his arm.

She was strong, and fit from years of exercise, but as she grabbed him he was as solid and unmoving as rock. She held on to him just above his elbow, knowing that he stopped and turned back because he chose to, not because of the pressure she was exerting on his arm.

'You can't marry me without my consent.' She looked up into his face and spoke through gritted teeth.

'I'll have your consent.'

'No, you won't!' Carrie said.

'I'll have *anything* I want.' He let his eyes sweep over her in a way that set her senses on red alert. But, despite the sense of danger, a dark ripple of anticipation shuddered through her.

He moved his arm slightly and Carrie suddenly realised she still had hold of him. His bicep bunched beneath her fingers, strong and powerfully sexy, making the nerves in her hand tingle in response.

'Is this about sex?' Carrie swallowed, letting her hand drop from his arm and taking a step backwards out of his reach. 'Did you propose just to get me into bed?'

'Don't be so naive,' Nik said darkly, edging forward. 'Why would I go to such lengths? You've always been easy prey—you've wanted me since the first moment we met in Darren's study.'

'No…no…that's not true,' Carrie stammered, backing away another step. Her heart was racing and her stomach was turning wild somersaults.

'It's nothing to be ashamed of.' Nik suddenly closed the gap between them and lifted his hands to cup the back of her head. 'It works both ways. I've wanted you since the beginning as well.'

'I don't want you!' Carrie protested, raising both arms to push his hands away from her head.

'Why fight it?' He caught her wrists, one in each hand, and held them above her head. She was locked in position, her arms in the air, her breasts pushing up towards him.

'Because you're a beast!' she cried. She tried to pull her hands down, to escape from his grip, but suddenly she became ultra-aware of how exposed her body felt with her arms above her head. A skitter of excitement ran through her, and her breasts started to throb. 'You lied to me, kidnapped me, and now you're threatening me!'

'But still I turn you on.' His voice, rich and deep, vibrated through her, setting off a reaction through her entire body.

'No!' She denied it passionately, but she couldn't suppress the compulsion to arch her back, thrusting her breasts closer to his chest. Her nipples felt hard as diamonds and were aching for him.

'Yes, I do,' he purred, leaning forward so that his chest brushed briefly against the points of her nipples, setting them on fire with the slightest contact, then withdrawing to leave them aching with frustration. 'You're desperate for my touch.'

'I'm not.' Her voice was a husky whisper and her body hummed with her pent-up desire for him.

'I'm going to touch you all over,' he said, tugging her

towards him so that her breasts rubbed against his chest again and a frisson of sexual excitement buzzed through her. 'I'm going to explore every inch of your body, find all the secret places that are yearning for my touch and make them mine.'

She squeezed her eyes shut, trying to ignore the sensations and desires that were storming her body, but it was impossible. Despite all the reasons why it would be a disaster to let Nikos Kristallis make love to her, there was nothing else in the world she could think about.

She wanted him to make love to her. She was desperate for him to make love to her.

'Don't fight it.' He released his hold on her wrists and started sliding his hands downwards, across the sensitive skin on the underside of her arms. Then his hands slid round to her back, and Carrie knew he was ready to pull her into his tight embrace. 'We both want this and I promise it will be good.'

She stared up at him, seeing his desire for her darkening his blue eyes. Her hands were clutching the front of his shirt, the fabric scrunched in her fists, and she realised she was pulling him towards her rather than pushing him away.

Then there was no more time for thought as his mouth came down on hers and suddenly he was kissing her with a fierce intensity.

She responded with a passion that equalled his, opening her lips and letting his tongue sweep into her mouth in a sensual invasion that took her breath away. Her mind was spinning and her body was trembling uncontrollably, but she clung to him, locked to his kiss as though nothing else mattered.

Their tongues moved together in a sensual dance, but the effects of the kiss extended far beyond the feelings created by their joined mouths. Waves of sensation washed through her whole body, making her reel from the intensity of it.

It was a soul-shattering kiss, a kiss that delved into her

very being and laid bare the shockingly powerful desire she felt for Nik.

She hardly noticed his hands moving as they skimmed across her body, but as they closed over her breasts her centre of awareness shifted immediately.

He held both breasts, cupping them gently in the palms of his hands. Then he started kneading the aching flesh through the fabric of her dress, teasing the jutting nipples with his thumbs.

The muscles in her neck felt weak, and as he pulled away from their kiss she let her head fall back, a sound of pure pleasure sighing from her open lips. It felt so good to feel his hands touching her, stroking her, sending wonderful feelings washing through her. But she yearned for more. She needed more.

Almost of their own volition her hands went to the buttons on her dress, undoing them—one, two, three—until Nik closed his hands over hers and pushed the top of her dress wide open. Her white bra had a front fastening, and in a second her breasts were free.

Nik bent down and took the throbbing peak of one breast in his mouth. She cried out and buried her hands in his hair, pulling him tightly to her. He responded by drawing the nipple deeply into his mouth, sucking harder and increasing the pressure of his caressing tongue.

A torrent of desire stormed through her, making her quiver and moan. An incredible pulsing of pure sexual energy started throbbing at the very core of her femininity, making her moan with pleasure and press her thighs tightly together.

She had never felt anything like it before, and was totally unprepared for the intensity of her own reaction. She felt herself swaying as her legs started to give way.

Nik swept her up into his arms and carried her over to the bed, where he laid her down. He sat beside her, leaning over her and looking down at her with blue eyes that were already dark with his rising passion. Excitement coiled through her and she started to tremble with anticipation. She couldn't just lie there, waiting for him to make a move, so she lifted her hands and grasped his shoulders to pull him down.

His arms were braced on either side of her body, but he let her tug him slowly down until his face hovered only inches above her own. His eyes were intense and he held her gaze for the longest moment, despite the fact that her hands were running wild all over his body, tugging his shirt free of his trousers and slipping underneath to touch his skin.

The heat of his body drew her like a magnetic attraction, and she slid her hands round to the front and started undoing his buttons. She wanted to see him naked, wanted to feel his naked body beneath her palms.

Then he pressed down, trapping her hands between their bodies, and kissed her. It was no gentle kiss, but a fierce and passionate conquest. His tongue plunged masterfully between her lips, thrusting into the soft interior of her mouth. She moved her tongue to meet his, and then they were writhing together in a kiss more erotic than Carrie had ever before experienced.

At last he lifted himself away slightly, allowing her hands to move freely again. She reached round him, smoothing her palms over the strong plains of his back, but he was on the move, suddenly kneeling over her, his hands on either side of her shoulders, one knee between her thighs and the other beside her hip. She was effectively pinned beneath him.

Her breath was coming in small, rapid gasps and she stared up at him hungrily, not caring that her desire for him must be completely obvious. He rocked forward, using his leg to nudge her dress up.

She gasped out loud as his long hard thigh brushed intimately between her legs, sending a jolt of pure sexual excitement thrilling through her. His expression intensified and he moved his leg again, letting it ride up and down between hers, all the time maintaining pressure on the place between her legs that was suddenly the very centre of her awareness.

A pulsing point of desire began to throb insistently where his thigh rubbed against her. She moaned with pleasure and looked up at him. She could see in his eyes that he wanted her, and if that wasn't enough she could feel his arousal, pressing hard and ready through the thin fabric of her summer dress.

She reached for him again, this time her hands finding the buckle of his belt. The leather was soft and flexible and she slipped the end through the loop. Suddenly he straightened up and he pushed her hands aside once more. He jerked the belt undone and quickly removed the rest of his clothes.

He stood naked beside the bed and she gazed up at his magnificent form appreciatively. She was torn between the desire to look and the need to touch, but she didn't have time for either as he quickly bent over her again and grasped her panties in his strong hands. With one swift movement he pulled them down and tossed them away.

Her heart thumped erratically as he knelt between her thighs. Her body was aching with her need for him, but at that last second she felt a rush of nervous energy. She wanted him. But this was something she'd never done before.

She looked up at him, gloriously naked above her, and, inexperienced as she was, her body knew what it wanted.

She needed to feel him moving inside her, and that need was growing greater every moment. She let her knees fall apart and reached to pull him down onto her, into her.

He hesitated, looking at her face as the hard tip of his penis pressed against her. She wriggled, unable to bear the delay, and lifted her hips towards him. At that moment he pressed forward, and as their bodies were finally joined she felt a sharp momentary pain.

He stopped suddenly, as if he had sensed what had happened, and looked down at her with an unreadable expression in his eyes.

The pain passed in a second, and as she felt her body ease to accommodate his hard masculine length she let out a long low moan of satisfaction.

But that was only the start. He began to move, and with each slow thrust a wave of pleasure crashed over her, spiralling out from the core of her womanhood to the tips of her fingers and beyond. It was wonderful. Her whole body trembled with delight, getting fuller and fuller with quivering, singing energy.

She was riding the moment, almost bursting with extraordinary sensation, moving closer and closer to the peak. Instinctively she lifted her knees towards her chest and angled her hips upwards, letting him thrust deeper and deeper into her. With every thrust she cried out, clinging to him, gripping his buttocks and holding him as tight to her as she could. His body was growing damp with sweat and her hands glided over his slick skin.

The pressure was building within her and she felt as if she would explode. She lifted her head, straining towards him, biting down on his neck as his head dipped next to hers.

Suddenly her moment came. Her toes curled, her breath caught in her throat and she felt her climax breaking over her like a tidal wave of sensation, pulsing through her body to every extremity. Her back arched and her head fell onto the pillow as she cried out his name. Aftershocks clenched inside her, and she felt her inner muscles tightening convulsively around his hardness, which was still moving deep inside her. The moment went on and on in an orgasm that was more powerful than anything she'd ever dreamed was possible.

Nik gave a shout and she knew his own climax was upon him. He reared back and was poised above her for a second as his body peaked in its moment of release. Then he collapsed onto her, breathing heavily in long ragged breaths.

She wrapped her arms around him, feeling his heart pounding against her breast, and let her body sink down into the bed, totally satisfied.

Nik lay there for a moment, feeling her body beneath his, feeling her still holding him inside.

He'd been right. Making love to Carrie had been good. No—*good* was not the right word. Incredible was a better way to describe it.

He lifted himself onto his elbows and rolled away so that he was beside her on the bed. He looked at her, waiting for his heart rate to slow, listening to the sound of her panting breaths slowly quieten.

She was lying supine next to him, still wearing her flowery summer dress, which was crumpled and mussed from their lovemaking. The front was slightly open, showing a glimpse of the shadow between her breasts, and the skirt was hiked up to her hips. She must have smoothed the hem down just enough to cover her decency when he moved off her, but her long legs were still gloriously naked.

She looked utterly irresistible, lying there in such wanton disarray, even though most of her body was still covered. In fact, apart from undoing the front of her bra, her panties were the only item of clothing that he'd removed. He remembered tearing them off and tossing them to one side, and was suddenly filled with an urgent desire to ravage her once more.

'Carrie,' he said, as a shaft of refreshed desire mixed with anger ripped through him, 'why didn't you tell me you were a virgin?'

CHAPTER EIGHT

'IT WAS none of your business.' Carrie pushed herself up into a sitting position and stared straight back at him. There was a defiant look on her flushed face, but deep in her green eyes he thought he could detect a glimmer of uncertainty.

'Of course it was,' he said.

An image of her strutting through the footballer's party, wearing that short red dress and those impossibly high-heeled sandals, flashed through his mind. No one who looked that sexy could be a virgin.

'No, it wasn't.' Carrie jumped off the bed and buttoned up the front of her dress. 'I didn't ask you how many lovers you've had before.'

'That's not the same thing,' Nik grated. 'And in any case I never misled you about my experience.'

He remembered all the times he'd kissed her. Her response had always been the same—as hot as hell. No timorous virgin could have been so full of desire for him.

'You're acting like I deprived you of something,' Carrie shot at him, her eyes flashing angrily.

'You lied to me.' He stood up and tugged his trousers on. 'And that will not be acceptable in the future.'

'I never lied,' Carrie said. 'You assumed.'

Nik looked at her, standing with her hands on her hips, staring straight back at him. Knowing that her bra was still undone under her dress and that she wasn't wearing any panties sent a powerful ache burning through him.

She was ripe and ready for picking, and he was the only man ever to have tasted the delights of her body. Now that she'd given herself to him, no other man would ever have her!

'We'll be married immediately,' he said.

'I'm not marrying you!' Carrie gasped. With everything that had just happened between them she'd almost forgotten the unbelievable proposal he'd made earlier. 'I never agreed to marry you!'

She bit her lip as she watched him pulling on his shirt. He couldn't really be serious about getting married, could he?

'I thought you'd understood the offer I made,' Nik said.

'It wasn't an offer,' Carrie replied, keeping her voice level. She had to keep her head and try to find a way out of this. 'It was blackmail.'

'Whatever you call it, the facts remain the same,' he said. 'Marry me and be a part of Danny's life—or leave and never see him again.'

'I'll fight you,' she said, hearing her voice rise as a jolt of panic ran through her. 'I'll get a lawyer.'

'Go ahead.' Nik turned away towards the door. 'Shall I send Irene to help you pack?'

'No!' She dashed across the room after him and was about to grab his arm to stop him when she remembered what had happened the last time she'd done that. At the last second she darted around him and stood with her back pressed against the closed door of the bedroom.

'You don't want to leave?' Nik said. 'I'm glad you're finally coming to your senses. It will be best for everyone.'

'No—we haven't finished our discussion yet,' Carrie said.

She held her arms stiffly by her sides and looked up into his face, determined not to feel overwhelmed by him.

But suddenly he seemed very large and powerful in front of her. He was too close for comfort, yet she knew she was the one who had slipped past him, positioning herself in his personal space.

'You know that your choices are severely limited,' Nik said, fixing her with intense blue eyes. 'I will not allow Danny to be taken off my property, which means that if you wish to seek legal representation you will have to leave him with me. I have no problem with that—but I'm surprised you are willing to abandon him. It doesn't add up with the dedication that you've always claimed you have for him.'

'I would never abandon Danny,' Carrie said, feeling her blood run cold at the thought of leaving Danny behind. She knew if she did that she might never see him again.

'Then you must agree to marry me.' He towered over her, making her shrink back against the door.

How had she managed to get in so deep with Nikos Kristallis? There was no way out that she could think of. He was so rich and powerful that she didn't stand a chance against him.

'I don't understand why we have to be married,' Carrie said, stalling for time. Maybe if she went along with him, made him trust her, she would be able to find a way to get Danny away from him. 'We hardly know each other. It wouldn't be a real marriage.'

'It will be real.' His blue eyes bored deep into her, starting a trembling at the very core of her body. 'Make no mistake that it will be a proper marriage in every sense and you will be expected to do *everything* a proper wife would do.'

'But why…?' Carrie faltered, pressing her teeth into her lower lip as she stared up at him with stormy green eyes.

Nik looked at her, watching the shifting emotions play across her beautiful features. She'd be no good at poker—everything she felt was always written on her face.

'Because it's best for my nephew,' he said, satisfied that he was finally getting her where he wanted.

'But what about my job?' Carrie asked in desperation.

'You won't need one once you are my wife,' Nik replied. 'I have more than enough to keep you and Danny in a comfortable lifestyle.'

'I don't understand what's in it for you,' she said, still determined to show she wasn't about to meekly accept whatever he told her.

'It's not about me,' he replied. 'As I just said—it's about what is best for Danny.'

'But how can it be good for him to be cared for by two people who don't even like each other?' she asked, bright spots of colour appearing on her cheeks as she spoke.

'I don't dislike you.' He took a step closer to her and slipped his hand under her hair, which was still slightly damp from her shower. He pushed it back over her shoulder, feeling a shiver run through her.

'It won't be a proper marriage.' She straightened her shoulders and met his eye boldly, but he knew she was thinking about what it would be like sharing a bed with him each and every night. 'People will know.'

'No one will know.' His voice was so low it was almost a growl, and he knew the warning in his words was clear. 'You will never do or say anything to reveal our arrangement. The purpose of our union is to protect Danny—so we will show the world that we are happily married.'

'Even real marriages are not always happy.' Carrie's voice shrank to little more than a whisper, but she continued to match his gaze.

'I don't intend my marriage to be a battlefield. I won't live that way,' he said. 'Be nice—or I may retract my offer.'

A spark of defiance flashed in her eyes at his provocative words, but Nik knew she had accepted the situation. Soon Carrie would be his—signed, sealed and delivered.

Carrie stared at the wedding band on her finger. The civil ceremony was over—she was Nik's wife.

It was two weeks since he'd demanded they be married, and for Carrie that time had passed in a haze of exhaustion and disbelief. At first all her energy had gone into caring for Danny. Then, when he'd got better, she'd tried to talk to Nik— but he'd seemed to work all the time. She'd wanted to be certain that she couldn't persuade him to change his mind, but he'd never been available. And now it was too late. They were husband and wife.

She watched the sunlight glinting off the gold ring, hardly able to believe she was married. Things had happened so quickly, and the only thing she'd had any say in was the choice of her wedding gown. It felt as if her life was totally out of her own control.

'You look beautiful,' Nik said, handing her a glass of champagne.

She glanced up in surprise and realised that they were alone. It was the first time since the day they'd made love. His eyes were intense as he met and held hers, and her heart started to beat faster.

'Thank you.' She knew her cheeks were colouring under his continuing gaze but she didn't look away. They were married now—man and wife. Suddenly everything seemed different, and she felt the flutter of nerves deep inside her.

'I believe there are ways we can make this work,' he said, leaning close to her ear and letting his lips brush tantalisingly against the sensitive skin of her neck.

His warm breath whispered in her hair and she shivered with pleasure, her mind suddenly whirling with memories of Nik making love to her. She'd never imagined that it could be such a totally overwhelming experience—especially not her first time.

'I want to lock the door and make love to you right now,' he murmured, tracing his hand slowly down her spine in a way that made the hairs on the back of her neck stand up and hot liquid desire pool deep inside.

'Wouldn't they all know what we're doing?' Her voice was shaky as she replied, but a powerful feeling of excitement was building up within her as she let herself lean against his hard masculine form.

Her body was suddenly humming with anticipation, longing to enjoy the wonders of Nik's lovemaking again. For the last two weeks she hadn't been able to put thoughts of it out of her mind.

'That wouldn't matter. We're married.' He took her champagne glass away from her, then lifted his hands to gently cup her face. 'But I have to go now.'

'What?'

Carrie pulled back and stared at him in shock. Had he really just said he was going now?

'I have pressing work commitments that I can't ignore,' Nik said.

'But…but surely not today?' Carrie gasped, feeling humiliated. She glanced out of the window as the unmistakable sound of an approaching helicopter filled the air.

'It's not what I would have wanted, but this is important.' He turned away from her and strode to the door.

By the time he was out of the room Nik's body was rigid with the effort needed not to turn back and seize her in his arms. He wanted to cancel his business meeting, even though he was in the final stages of an important acquisition he'd been working on for ever. Right now it seemed less important than taking Carrie to bed.

It wasn't like him. He was a red-blooded male with a healthy appetite for women—but he'd always known when to put business before sex. Somehow Carrie had got under his skin, making him want to do things he wouldn't normally do.

Five days later Nik had still not returned to the villa. Carrie sat on the tree-top balcony, feeding Danny his breakfast and wondered just what she'd got herself into.

Nik had said he wanted to be part of Danny's life, that he wanted their marriage to appear normal—but he wasn't here. What if he never returned? What if he simply left her locked up here, like a princess in a tower?

She frowned, looking out at the pure blue sky and the glittering azure sea in the bay below her. It was time to stop waiting for Nik.

It was a beautiful Mediterranean day and she'd take Danny and go exploring. They'd already investigated every nook and cranny of the villa's beautiful garden, but now she decided to go further afield. She'd take the path that she'd discovered led down to a private beach far below.

She knocked back the last of her juice and lifted Danny out of his highchair.

'Let's go.' She smiled at him. 'Are you going to walk a little bit today?' She held his hands and guided him along in his funny, bouncy tiptoeing walk. He'd been pulling himself up to stand, even 'cruising' around the room, hanging onto the furniture, for a month or so, but he'd shown no real desire to actually walk yet.

Half an hour later Carrie set off along the winding path, finding it a delightful walk down a wooded slope to the beach.

The going was steep, and she was glad of the three-wheeler buggy that Irene had produced from somewhere, but the tantalising glimpses of sparkling sea would have drawn her on even if she'd had to carry Danny and the very heavy bag.

It was wonderful to be out and about on her own with Danny, and in hardly any time at all she turned one last bend and there in front of her was a gorgeous curve of beach and the glittering blue sea. But right across the path there was a tall wrought-iron gate, blocking her way.

She stopped in her tracks and stared at it. Was it locked? Would she have to turn back? At that moment the gate swung soundlessly inward on well-oiled hinges, and Carrie noticed the little camera and voice grid mounted on the gatepost.

'Thank you!' she called, looking up at the camera and smiling as she recalled Nik's words about the best security system. No doubt cameras covered the beach as well—their usual purpose being to prevent intruders making their way onto Kristallis property, but on this occasion to stop her trying to flag down a passing boat in an attempt to sail away with Danny.

The idea suddenly struck her as funny. Despite Nik's comment in the limousine she knew that the security system hadn't really been set up to keep her prisoner, but she had the sudden childish impulse to start acting suspiciously for the benefit of the cameras, just to see what would happen.

At that moment Danny squealed, and started wriggling against his harness. She'd never taken him to a beach before, and his eyes were round and bright as he stared out at the exciting terrain.

She pushed the buggy through the gate and found herself at the top of a few steps down to the beach. The steps were wide and sloping and, being constructed of sun-bleached olive wood packed with silvery grey pebbles, were in perfect sympathy with the unspoilt beach. They looked as if they'd been there for years.

Carrie stooped to lift Danny out of his seat, and a moment later she was crunching across the narrow beach towards the sea, with Danny's cries of excitement tickling her cheek.

'Isn't it lovely?' she murmured, quietly absorbing the subtle beauty of the setting. It truly was a charming bay, with a sweeping arc of silver pebbles giving way to a strip of rich golden sand that was gently lapped by the water. At each end of the small bay precipitous ochre cliffs plunged into the peacock-blue sea, and behind her the wooded slopes rose up steeply, enclosing her in a beautiful secluded paradise.

If she'd wanted a shady spot she could have settled under the branches of the wizened old olive trees that edged the beach, but she was enjoying the feel of the sun on her skin too much. She put Danny down and sat beside him, letting her fingers close over a warm flat pebble. All the pebbles seemed to be perfectly smooth, perfectly round—perfect for skimming.

With a dip of her body and a flick of her wrist she flipped the pebble out over the sea. One bounce, two bounces and it disappeared under the water with a plop.

Danny let out an excited squeal and grabbed up a handful of pebbles to launch at the sea himself.

'Oh, dear.' She smiled wryly. 'I probably shouldn't be teaching you to throw stones!' But even though she knew she shouldn't, she just couldn't resist it.

A few minutes later, encouraged by Danny's enthusiastic response, she was standing up and practising her skimming skills. It was ages since she'd skimmed stones, and try as she might she couldn't manage more than two bounces.

Suddenly a stone whizzed past her shoulder and tripped across the water. One, two, three, four, five bounces, before breaking the surface and sinking down into the clear sea.

She gasped and looked round, to see Nik standing on the beach behind her.

He was smiling broadly. It was a heart-stoppingly gorgeous expression she'd never seen him show before, and suddenly butterflies started to flutter in her stomach.

She smiled back, instinctively matching the warmth in his expression, and a surge of excitement ran through her. She'd spent the last five days resenting his absence, but somehow his smile had the power to lift her mood. All at once she was brimming with memories of their lovemaking, and she let her eyes run over him with a buzz of pure pleasure.

He was wearing worn jeans and a tight black T-shirt and he looked simply incredible. He was dressed more casually than she'd ever seen him before, but the look really suited him—the short sleeves showing off the well-defined muscles of his arms, the snug jeans emphasising the lean athletic strength of his long legs.

'Hello,' he said, still smiling. 'How are you? How's Danny?'

'We're fine.' Carrie suddenly found it a challenge to bring her thoughts into any kind of order as his blue eyes caught hold of hers. 'He's full of beans today.'

'That's good,' Nik replied. 'I've always liked it here.' He knelt down next to them and leant forward to catch Danny's attention. 'Hello, what have you been doing?'

Carrie watched them with a curious feeling spreading through her. As far as she could remember Nik had never spoken directly to Danny before. It seemed as if he actually wanted to engage properly with his nephew for the first time.

'Um…learning to throw stones,' Carrie said awkwardly.

'Everyone likes to throw stones into water,' Nik said with a shrug, still maintaining eye contact with the baby. 'We'll just have to teach you to be careful when people are around, won't we?'

Danny grinned and lifted his arms, as if he wanted Nik to pick him up. Nik glanced over at Carrie, then reached out and swung Danny up into his arms.

'Let's walk.' He stood up and set out along the strip of golden sand that edged the gently lapping water.

Carrie walked behind them, feeling even more unsettled than before. It was good that Nik was making an effort with Danny, wasn't it? So why did she feel so strange about it? She'd married Nik for Danny's sake—she ought to be pleased that he was starting to form a relationship with him.

'I used to skim stones with my brother,' Nik said over his shoulder, slowing down until she fell into step beside him. 'We were always very competitive about it.'

'I'm not very good at it,' Carrie replied, realising that it was the first time Nik had spoken about Leonidas in a personal way. He was full of surprises today—it was making her feel jittery.

'We practised a lot,' Nik said. 'We both wanted to be the best.'

'On this beach?' Carrie asked, wondering about their childhood. Leonidas had been determined that Danny should have a very different childhood from his strict Greek upbringing with his overbearing father.

'No, but it was a very similar beach, on my parents' property on the mainland,' Nik replied. 'I bought this place a few years ago, for times when I need to get away from the city.'

Carrie bit her lip and looked at Nik. Talking about his family had reminded her of something that had been bothering her for some time, but she didn't know how he would react if she brought it up.

'How is it that you didn't know about Danny until just a few weeks ago?' she asked, steeling herself for his response.

Nik stopped abruptly and turned towards her. In the bright morning light his blue eyes were more vibrant than ever, but there was a hint of unknown emotion clouding their depths.

'I hadn't spoken to my brother for some time.' His expression was uncharacteristically troubled. 'I didn't know he had married your cousin, let alone had a child with her. I didn't find out about his death until after the funeral.'

'But your father knew. He came to the funeral,' Carrie said, shuddering at the memory of how unpleasant Cosmo had been. 'And he definitely knew about Danny.'

'He didn't tell me,' Nik said simply. 'He only told me Leonidas had died—and not until after the funeral.'

'I don't understand why he'd keep such important news from you,' Carrie said. But even before she'd finished speaking she knew why. Cosmo had not wanted to acknowledge Danny as a Kristallis. He must have known there would be a chance that Nik would want his brother's son to be part of the family.

'My father was a difficult man,' Nik replied, giving no clue as to whether he had realised his father's motivation in keeping Danny a secret.

Carrie waited, hoping he'd carry on speaking. She wanted to know how their family had got so messed up that two brothers hadn't spoken for years and their father had rejected his own grandson. She knew Leonidas's side of the story—at least up until he had left Greece—but she wanted to hear Nik explain it.

There was a long pause, but he didn't continue. In the end she broke the silence, hoping that if she shared information about her childhood he would follow suit.

'*My* father isn't easy to get along with,' she said. 'All through my childhood I tried to get to know him, but I always ended up disappointed.'

'What happened?' Nik asked.

Carrie looked at him and thought he seemed genuinely interested to hear about her background. Somehow she had the feeling he usually avoided that sort of personal discussion—but maybe he was prepared to make an exception for his wife.

'When I was growing up he always seemed to take jobs as far away as possible—he's a marine engineer, and his work took him all round the world. My aunt and uncle disapproved, saying he could get a job closer to home if he wanted. They called him a workaholic and said he'd rather put his work before his daughter.' She paused and took a deep breath. 'I knew they never really wanted me, but they gladly banked the cheques Dad sent for my upkeep. I felt like I was being looked after for money.'

'That must have been hard,' Nik said.

'It was.' Carrie gazed at the wooded mountain slope on the other side of the bay, but she was thinking about her childhood in England. 'He let me down so many times. He never remembered my birthday or anything important. I just wanted to talk to him—but he was never there.'

'Do you see him now?' Nik asked.

'Rarely.' Carrie turned back to Nik. His blue eyes were serious. 'It got easier to deal with once I'd left home, once I was independent. When I was eighteen I got a small inheritance from my mother. It was enough for a deposit on my flat in London, and I started working in the fitness industry. I'd always been keen on sport—it was a good way to escape for a while.'

Nik was still looking at her, listening carefully to what she was saying. She got the feeling he understood how difficult her childhood had been at times.

'My father was always conscious of his duty as a good father. And he made sure Leonidas and I knew our duty as his sons.' Nik took a breath, almost as if he'd startled himself by talking about his family. 'My father never missed any significant dates—I imagine his secretary sent him a memo—but neither of us were ever able to talk to him.'

'Leonidas said he only ever wanted to hear about your successes at school or other achievements that proved you were living up to the Kristallis name,' Carrie said. 'Leonidas didn't want Danny to grow up judged only by how successful he was. It was something I had in common with your brother,' she continued, her voice suddenly shaky. 'We both knew what it was like to have a father who didn't really care about us. Leonidas wanted Danny to grow up knowing he was loved, feeling able to talk about anything.'

She stopped walking and looked across at the child in Nik's arms. She knew Nik had seen her eyes sparkling with tears.

'I share that desire too,' he said quietly. 'That is why I came for Danny—he needs a decent father figure.'

'You still haven't answered the question I asked,' Carrie pressed. She blinked away unshed tears and started to walk along the beach again. 'If your father didn't tell you, how did you find out abut Danny?'

'Going through my father's personal papers after he died,' Nik said. 'There was a lot to sort through, but as soon as I found references to Leonidas's son I turned my attention to following the trail that led to you.'

'I'm glad you did,' Carrie said.

Suddenly she stopped stock-still, aware that she'd just said something momentous.

'I meant…I meant that…' She stumbled over the words. 'I don't mean that I approve of the way you brought us here to Corfu—it was underhand and unacceptable— but I do accept that it's good for Danny to get to know his father's brother.'

Nik stopped abruptly beside her and turned to fix her with a powerful stare. The atmosphere between them was suddenly super-charged.

'Carrie…' His voice throbbed with intensity. 'We have to move past the events that led us to this time and place. We can't change what has happened—but we *can* make a good life for Danny.'

'I know,' she replied, trying to keep the words steady despite the sudden pounding of her heart. They were standing beside the vast open space of a calm sea—but at that moment she felt as if she was enclosed with Nik in a small stormy space.

'If I could go back and change what happened to Leonidas and Sophie I would,' Nik said. 'But that was out of my control. More than anything I wish I had not ignored what was in my control. I should have put things right between us before Leonidas died.'

Carrie stared at him, overwhelmed by the depth of feeling that coloured his voice. He'd always seemed so controlled when talking about his brother, but now he was showing real emotion.

'What happened between you?' she asked in a small voice.

'It was after my mother died,' Nik explained. 'She was the one person who kept our family together. Just like your father, my father lived and breathed his work. Kristallis Industries was everything to him, and he had no time for his family.' He paused and took a breath. 'My mother eased the tensions between us. She softened my father and kept Leonidas from overreacting when he couldn't see eye to eye with him.'

'What happened after she died?' Carrie prompted quietly.

'Leonidas was grief-struck—we all were,' Nik said. 'He had a blazing row with my father—I can't even remember what it was about—which ended with him storming off, saying he wanted nothing more to do with our family.'

'Did you try to talk to him?' Carrie asked gently.

'We argued,' Nik said. 'I accused him of taking the easy way out. I accused him of showing no respect for my mother's memory—she had dedicated years to keeping the family together, and as soon as she was gone he was ready to walk out.'

'It must have been a terrible time,' Carrie said. She knew

how forceful and single-minded all three of the Kristallis men could be.

After Leonidas had married her cousin she had grown to love him, but he had always displayed a fiery Greek temper. Her one encounter with Cosmo had told her all she needed to know about *his* personality. And she knew from first-hand experience how ruthlessly Nik operated to get what he wanted.

She shuddered, imagining the fireworks that must have flown when the three Kristallis men had clashed.

'I have to head back to the villa now.' Nik's voice jolted her out of her thoughts.

'But…but you've only just got here,' she stammered, surprising herself with how much she wanted Nik to spend more time with them. 'Why do you have to go so soon?'

'Work,' Nik said shortly, passing Danny over to Carrie. 'It's unavoidable.' He was already crunching away across the pebbles to the gate.

CHAPTER NINE

CARRIE leant over the cot and brushed her fingertips lightly over Danny's hair. He looked blissfully content as he slept, and her heart swelled with her love for him.

She crossed the room and walked onto the balcony overlooking the mountainside that dipped down to the bay. The sun was setting, and she gazed out at a sea that looked like molten gold. It was a beautiful view, but it didn't improve her mood.

She hadn't seen Nik again since that morning—apparently he was still working—and she'd begun to worry about what her life would be like, married to him. She was really starting to feel like a pampered princess locked up in a tower. All the material things she could want were provided for her—but she didn't have her freedom. Danny would need to make friends with other children, and she needed contact with other people. She was missing her job and friends at home.

When it came right down to it, she had to admit that being ignored by Nik was hurting her feelings. That walk along the beach had seemed special to her—it had felt as if they were finally making a connection—but to him it had obviously been just something he had to fit in around his work.

Growing up, it had been hard for Carrie to come to terms with the fact that her occasional visits with her father had had to be fitted in around his work. She didn't like the thought that she was in the same situation with Nik.

She decided then and there that the next time she saw Nik she would challenge him on the subject. She had started to hope that there was a way they could work together to bring up Danny—but if he was never there what was the point of being married at all?

A slight noise coming from inside caught her attention, and she turned to see what it was. Nik was leaning over the cot, looking down at Danny.

A ripple of emotion passed through her and she bit her lip, staring at him. Why did she feel so pleased to see him when she'd spent most of the day feeling angry with him for the way he'd been ignoring her?

He looked up and, seeing her watching him through the open door, he smiled. Before she could help it she'd smiled back, suddenly realising that she had missed him. Why did his smile have the power to make her bad mood drift away?

But as he walked towards her she remembered her intention to make him talk about the future. She folded her arms, determined not to let him charm her with a dazzling smile, and tried to make her expression stern.

'I'm sorry.' He held his hands out in an open gesture as he approached her. 'I've left you alone too long and I want to make it up to you.'

'It's not enough just to say sorry,' Carrie said, determined not to be distracted from her good intentions to sort things out between them. 'I don't want to just sit around here waiting for you to spare us a few minutes out of your work schedule. I need to build a proper life for Danny and me. And that involves going out and meeting people, being part of the community, maybe getting a part-time job as a personal trainer…'

'There's no hurry to talk about that now.' Nik took a step

forward and lifted his hand to brush a strand of hair back from her face.

As his fingers touched her skin a tremor ran through her, and suddenly it was hard for her to be aware of anything other than Nik standing right in front of her.

'We can't put this conversation off.' Carrie tried to sound firm, but her words came out in a breathless rush. 'You'll be gone again in the morning, and I won't see you again for days.'

'It'll be all right.' Nik bent to press his lips against the side of her neck. 'My business deal is completed so we can talk about it tomorrow. I'm not going anywhere.'

'But I want to get things sorted out,' Carrie said, sucking in a wobbly breath as Nik opened his mouth against her neck and started trailing his tongue downwards. She was wearing a strappy sundress and his fingers skimmed lightly over the naked skin of her shoulder in a way that made shivers skitter down her spine. She took a step backwards and found the backs of her legs pressed against one of the balcony chairs.

'Tomorrow.' Nik's breath tickled her skin, making little darts of pleasure tremble through her. 'I give you my word, we'll talk properly tomorrow.'

She opened her mouth to speak, but at that moment Nik's mouth closed over hers. His tongue slipped in through her parted lips and all her thoughts were suddenly forgotten.

He kissed her gently, tenderly exploring the soft recesses of her mouth. It wasn't the hot, furious conquest of their previous kisses, but a long, slow-burning seduction.

Despite the change of pace she was soon clinging breathlessly to him, her whole body quivering with reawakened sensations, until at last he pulled back and she gazed up at him wordlessly. The setting sun was behind him, casting his handsome face into shadow, but still he looked incredible.

'I'm going to make love to you,' he said quietly, looking

at her with such intensity that a flurry of excitement started deep in her stomach. 'Think of this as the wedding night we didn't have.'

'You're making my legs feel weak.' She'd meant to sound light and breezy, but the words came out as a husky murmur that made his eyes darken with heightened desire.

'Then you'd better sit down,' he said, sweeping her off her feet and lowering her onto a chair. 'Because soon you won't be able to stand.'

Carrie gasped, and was about to protest when he stopped her words with another long languorous kiss. His tongue slid against hers, unhurried and sensuous in its movements, like a sultry slow dance that was simmering with the promise of a passionate release still to come.

He was kneeling beside her chair. One arm was around her shoulders, locking her to his kiss, and the other hand was skimming her body with a light, teasing touch. At last his fingers came to rest quite deliberately under the hem of her dress, halfway up her inner thigh. He pulled back from the kiss to look at her.

Carrie gazed at him, feeling slightly bemused. Her whole being was humming with sexual readiness and all she could think about was what it would feel like when he touched her intimately.

His hand on her leg started to move inexorably upwards, towards the place in her body that was already throbbing out its need for him. Her legs fell apart and she held her breath, waiting for his fingertips to make contact with her aching flesh.

'Last time we made love I was negligent,' he said, finally reaching the very top of her inner thigh. At the last moment, just when she was poised on the edge of glorious anticipation, waiting to feel his masterful touch, his fingers took a diversion upwards towards her left hip. 'These were the only items of your clothing that I removed.' He hooked his thumb under the elastic of her panties. 'I won't be so rash again. You can rest assured that it will be a long time before I remove these tonight.'

Carrie's breath came out in a shuddering sigh. She hardly had time to react to his announcement before he pushed her dress upwards and dropped his head to scatter kisses on her naked stomach. Somehow he had manoeuvred himself so that he knelt between her parted thighs, and as he leant forward she felt both exposed and overwhelmingly excited.

Once again he pulled away and sat back on his heels, looking up at her. She gazed down at his face, hardly able to believe what was happening. The most gorgeous man in the world—the only man she had ever felt this way about—was kneeling between her legs, making love to her in the most unexpected, marvellous way.

'Your skin is glowing in the sunset,' he murmured, lifting his hands to the front buttons of her dress. 'I want to see your naked breasts touched by the golden sunlight.'

'My skin is glowing because of you,' Carrie breathed, sitting almost mesmerised while he undid her dress and slipped his hands behind her to unfasten the strapless bra she wore.

'You are like a golden goddess.' He cupped her breasts tenderly, looking at her with the most open and adoring expression.

'Normally I'm pale,' Carrie said, brimming with delight at his extravagant flattery. She wasn't used to playing sensual word games, and it filled her with a heady excitement. 'Perhaps you'd prefer a bronzed Greek beauty?' she asked, and suddenly felt a moment's insecurity.

'No, I like your white skin,' he said. 'I want to see it shimmering like a pearl in the moonlight.'

'Don't look now, then,' she teased, filled with an unaccustomed sexual confidence as she arched her back and flourished her breasts at him before pulling her dress closed.

'Oh, yes,' he murmured as he pushed her dress apart again and leant forward to nuzzle her breasts. 'I intend to look at you and touch you and keep you here until the moon is well into the night sky.'

'Someone may come,' she gasped, looking over Nik's head along the darkening balcony.

'No one will disturb us, I promise,' he said. Then his mouth closed over her nipple.

CHAPTER TEN

A SIGH of delight escaped Carrie's parted lips and her head fell back. She gazed with unfocussed eyes at the bougainvillea, sprawling luxuriously over the balcony, the scarlet flowers shining like little Christmas lanterns in the last rays of the setting sun.

Nik's tongue was drawing circles around her nipple, eliciting the most wonderful sensations that spiralled out and filled her whole body with a magical glow. His hand caressed her other breast and his arm was behind her, holding her safe and secure as she sat on the chair.

Her eyelids slid down and she gave herself over completely to Nik's lovemaking. His fingers deftly managed the last of her buttons and she felt the warm evening breeze whispering across her naked skin. His mouth followed, exploring parts of her body that until that moment she had never realised were so sensitive.

She felt herself trembling as the sensations within her slowly built. His touch was so gentle, but her desire for him was growing more and more powerful.

'You're cold,' he said, scooping her up into his strong arms and crossing to the door of her bedroom before his words had fully penetrated the glorious cocoon of sensuality in which he'd wrapped her.

'No,' she said. 'You're keeping me warm.' She smiled up at him languidly as he laid her carefully on the bed.

'You are so beautiful.' His voice was gruff as he looked down at her beneath him, dressed in nothing but her white lacy panties.

'And you are wearing too many clothes,' she responded, marvellously free of inhibition as she rolled onto her side to watch him undress.

'Well, I can soon put that right.' He stripped off his clothes swiftly, all the while letting his eyes roam appreciatively over her naked curves.

Suddenly a feeling of pure sexual excitement shuddered through Carrie. Nik was making love to her, and all the wonderful feelings she had already experienced were only the very start of what was to come.

'Kiss me,' she said huskily, rising to her knees and wrapping her arms around him as soon as he moved within her reach.

His tongue plunged between her lips, and at that moment the tempo of their foreplay increased. He was just as aware of her needs, but gone were the long slow strokes of his fingertips, the gentle feather-light brushes of his lips. Now he was making love to her with an urgency that matched her own heightened arousal.

His lips were demanding on hers, and he pushed her down onto the bed purposefully, his hand sliding across her stomach and under the lace of her panties. Then his fingers dipped deep, finding the place that craved his attention.

At first he stroked gently, circling back and forth with the lightest of touches. Soon she was trembling in his arms, breathing rapidly and yearning for more.

Carrie whimpered as he suddenly increased the intensity of his touch. She closed her eyes and pressed her head back against the soft pillow, giving in to the wonderful feelings that his touch created. Her body arched and vibrated, tingling with an exquisite pleasure that reached every extremity.

His mouth closed, hot and demanding, over her nipple. He worked the aching peak with his tongue and she cried out in surprise as overwhelming sensations coursed through her body.

Her breath was coming in gasps and moans and she writhed on the bed. Nik's fingers still toyed with her, stroking her on to new heights, unrelenting as he followed her movements whilst she bucked her hips and arched her back.

'Oh! Oh!' she gasped. 'I... I...' She couldn't speak as wave after wave of pleasure crashed over her. Her world was rocking and she clung to Nik for support, carried away on the rush of excitement that exploded within her. His arms swooped her up and he held her shuddering body next to his chest.

Slowly she became aware that he was breathing as raggedly as her, then he laid her gently back against the pillows. Her body was still humming from his touch, and as he paused by her feet and kissed her toes she could feel the results of his caresses quivering through her body. Each brush of his hand or touch of his mouth set her body trembling anew.

'I think it's time to remove these.' He let his fingertips trace the patterns on the lace of her panties, but his touch was light and teasing, driving Carrie almost to distraction with her urgent desire for him. She needed to feel him strong and powerful, filling her with his hard male flesh.

'I want you!' she cried out. She couldn't wait any longer. She pulled her panties off herself and reached for him. 'I need you *now*!'

Nik groaned, a deep animal rumble, and quickly moved over her. He paused for a moment, looking down at her with hungry eyes.

She lay beneath him, suddenly desperate to feel him inside her. Her trembling body ached for him. He had made her ready— more than ready—and now she needed him like she'd never needed anything before. She slipped her hands down his back to his hard buttocks and grasped him firmly, urging him on.

He pressed his hips down, his hard male flesh sliding smoothly into the place that was so desperately aching to be filled. Then he began to rock against her, pushing in and pulling out. He took it slowly at first, but each movement sent a delicious wave of pleasure rushing through her.

Carrie moaned and clung to his back, tilting her hips to bring them even closer. She heard his breath coming in short hot gasps that matched her own, each breath escaping in time with every powerful thrust. The intensity was building, his pace increasing. He pushed into her harder and faster, each movement filling her with pleasure.

Overwhelming sensations coursed through her. Her body was quivering, from the tips of her fingers to the ends of her toes. Incredible feelings spiralled within her, shimmering out from the glorious place where they were joined to the tingling peaks of her breasts.

Without breaking his rhythm Nik eased away slightly, allowing space for his hand to slip down between them. His thumb found her sensitive bud, caressed it lightly.

Carrie cried out. Her body splintered into a million points of pleasure that lifted her beyond anything she had ever imagined. Gasping and trembling, she clung to Nik.

A second later she heard him cry out too, shuddering and panting as he reached his explosive climax.

'I'm glad I waited until I had time to spend with you properly,' Nik murmured some time later, as he traced his fingers along her collarbone and leant over to dip his tongue gently into the hollow at the base of her throat.

Carrie smiled when he raised his head to look into her face. She lifted her hand and smoothed her palm against his cheek. Everything seemed different now, she thought, gazing lovingly into the face of the man with whom she had just shared the most magical experience.

A sense of intimacy still lingered between them, as if to prove the act of lovemaking had been more than just a physical experience. Her body glowed with the aftermath of his loving, but she also felt a powerful connection had been forged between them. Surely everything would turn out all right now? Surely they would be able to find a way forward that suited everyone?

'It's been a busy few weeks,' Nik said, lying propped up on his side next to her, gently caressing the swell of her hip with his fingertips. 'But I've worked hard to clear some space for us. There will be time to discuss all the issues you mentioned earlier.'

'Thank you,' Carrie said. She smiled with relief, believing he meant what he said. There was a lot on her mind, and she needed to know where she stood, but at that moment all she could think about was the feel of Nik's fingers on her skin.

'It's important to me that you and Danny feel you belong here,' he said, letting his hand slide upwards until he held her breast softly in his palm. 'This is your home now, and you must have whatever you need.'

The glimmer in his eyes told her exactly what he thought she needed right then. And if that message wasn't clear enough he pulled her back into his arms and kissed her.

The following morning Carrie was in fine spirits as she walked down the winding path to the cove below the villa. Nik was with her. He was pushing Danny's buggy and they were all going to the beach together.

She'd made that same walk with Danny only yesterday, but now everything had changed. The sense of closeness she had felt with Nik the previous night was still there, wrapping her in a warm and comfortable glow. They'd all enjoyed breakfast together on the balcony, and for the first time she felt as if they were truly becoming a family.

'Last night you said there were a lot of things you wanted to talk about.' Nik flashed a smile at her as he spoke, and in the dappled shade under the olive trees he looked utterly gorgeous. He turned his attention back to pushing Danny safely over the uneven ground, but he inclined his head slightly, waiting for her response.

'Yes, there were…I mean there are.' Carrie gazed at him, suddenly finding it difficult to remember what had seemed so pressing the night before. Right then she just wanted to enjoy the moment, with Nik and Danny.

'You mentioned that Danny needs friends his own age,' Nik said. 'I have several cousins with a number of young children.'

'Oh,' Carrie said, thrown slightly off her stride by the discovery that Danny apparently had a lot of Greek relatives.

'But I thought it would be best if *we* spent some time together first—getting to know each other better before rushing into any family gatherings,' Nik said. 'Unless you think he needs contact with other children sooner?'

'No, no.' Carrie felt disproportionately relieved at Nik's intention to wait. 'Your plan not to rush into anything seems sensible.'

'I know he'll need other friends, too,' Nik added with a smile. 'Not just Kristallis children. We'll look into it.'

'Thank you,' Carrie said, just as they turned the corner and arrived at the wrought-iron gate to the beach. The gate swung open without a squeak, and they walked through onto the silver pebble steps.

It was a beautiful Mediterranean day. The sea was a gorgeous peacock-blue beneath a cloudless sky, and the olive trees on the slopes that flanked the bay shimmered in the sunlight.

'Let's go down to the water,' Nik said, lifting Danny out of his buggy and crunching off across the smooth pebbles.

Carrie followed along behind them, having difficulty keeping up with Nik's long stride as Danny's noisy enthusiasm drove him swiftly on towards the sea.

He stopped as he reached the strip of golden sand that edged the water and, kicking his shoes off, turned back to throw her a dazzling smile.

Carrie's heart turned over and she stopped in her tracks. The warmth of his smile spread over her, sinking right into her soul, filling her with happiness. It felt so good just to be standing there—smiling back at him, gazing deeply into his blue eyes.

She'd never felt that way before. She'd never been so absurdly happy just to smile at someone. Never felt someone's smile enfold her like a wonderful embrace.

The moment could have lasted for ever, but suddenly Danny made an unexpected lunge towards the water.

'Whoa! What are you up to?' Nik laughed, breaking eye contact with Carrie and hoisting Danny up more tightly in his arms.

'He likes the water,' Carrie said distractedly. Why had sharing a simple smile with Nik made her feel so strange?

'He wants to get wet!' Nik exclaimed. 'I'll take his shoes off and splash his feet.'

Carrie pushed her fringe back off her face and brought her attention back to the situation at hand. 'You'll have a hard time only getting his feet wet, but Irene packed a change of clothes, so don't worry too much.'

Nik sat down on the pebbles, rolled up Danny's trousers and pulled off his shoes and socks. He stuffed them into his pockets and rose smoothly to his feet, despite the shifting pebbles beneath him, and started making his way along the water's edge, dipping Danny up and down so that his toes skimmed the water.

Carrie let her eyes run appreciatively across Nik's broad back and powerful shoulders as he lifted Danny easily up and down over the lapping waves. The movement of his well-defined muscles under the tight black fabric of his T-shirt snared her gaze, making her heart start to beat a bit faster. She remembered so well how those muscles felt beneath her questing hands, as he lay on top of her, making love to her.

Her gaze slipped lower and she found herself admiring the athletic grace of his long stride. Then suddenly she was thinking about how those strong legs felt lying between hers. She remembered gripping his buttocks tightly, urging him on, pulling him deeper as he thrust inside her.

Her body trembled as echoes of the sensations that had overwhelmed her so magically rippled through her. She longed to feel that way again, to lie in Nik's arms night after night.

'The water's not that warm yet,' Nik said over his shoulder, speaking loudly to be heard over Danny's squeals of delight. 'But you'll really love it here in the summer. It will be perfect then. In July and August the water is as warm as a bath, but the olive groves are cool and shady.'

Carrie stopped walking and looked at him, feeling momentarily confused. She'd been so preoccupied thinking about making love to Nik that she wasn't entirely sure what he had just said.

He turned, still holding her with his eyes, and retraced his steps so that he was standing right in front of her. He lifted one hand and brushed his fingers across her temple, tucking the loose tendrils of hair back behind her ear. An automatic shiver ran through her, and she inclined her head to rest her cheek against his open palm. She returned his gaze, drifting dreamily in the blue depths of his eyes.

'You look tired,' he said, leaning forward to place a gentle kiss on her lips. 'Sit down and rest for a few minutes while I play with Danny.'

She gazed back at him, pleasantly surprised by the tenderness of his kiss and slightly taken aback by his words. But it was true—she did feel unusually tired.

'All right,' she said. 'Just for a few minutes.' She released his eyes reluctantly and turned to walk back up the beach a few paces, to a place where the smooth pebbles formed a natural mound that looked comfortable for sitting on.

Nik smiled at her, as if her actions pleased him, then went back to dipping Danny up and down over the gently lapping water.

It was an enchanting bay, enclosed on both sides by cliffs and backed by the steep wooded slopes. The sea was a blissful shade of blue and the barest touch of a breeze ruffled her hair deliciously.

But the beautiful view didn't hold her attention. All she wanted to do was feast her eyes on Nik, soaking up everything about the way he looked, the way he moved.

Just watching him made a funny feeling start to spread through her—and she wasn't thinking about making love to him. Just being near him made her feel happy, and seeing him play so naturally with Danny filled her with hope for the future. He'd make a very good father for Danny. And for his own child one day in the future, if things worked out between them.

Carrie gasped and clamped her hand over her mouth. She'd been in Corfu for three weeks and she hadn't had a period. Nik had made love to her the day after they'd arrived and they hadn't used any protection.

She was pregnant!

An icy shiver ran through her and she hugged herself, despite the heat of the Greek sun.

She *might* be pregnant, she told herself sternly, trying to keep calm. She'd buy a pregnancy test, and then she'd know for sure.

But how could she get a pregnancy test? Nik had her locked up here like his prisoner. She wasn't allowed off his property. She couldn't even go to a shop and buy a test.

A nasty mixture of anger and despair coiled through her, making her feel sick to her stomach. That was a sure sign of pregnancy, she thought bitterly, ignoring the fact that she hadn't felt sick a minute earlier.

She'd always wanted a child of her own, and had hoped that one day she'd be able to give Danny a little playmate. But not like this. It was too soon.

Nik controlled everything—Danny's life, her life. He even controlled her ability to discover whether or not she was pregnant. If she had a baby she'd be putting herself more completely under his control.

What if it didn't work out between them? If he wouldn't give up on Danny, his brother's child, he'd never, *ever* give up on his own child. He'd take Carrie's child away from her as brutally as he'd forced her into marrying him to get possession of Danny.

She stared at Nik balefully. A moment ago she'd been filled with happiness while she watched him playing with Danny. Now her insides were filled with a horrible churning mess of emotions. She had to find out whether or not she was pregnant.

'I need to go shopping,' she called out to Nik. She started to get up, but her legs felt unaccountably weak so she stayed sitting down, staring up at him as he turned and walked towards her.

'I'll take you after lunch.' Nik was studying her carefully through narrowed eyes, a questioning expression on his face.

'I want to go on my own,' she said, squinting up at him in the bright reflected sunlight. She suddenly wished she had her sunglasses on. She didn't like the feeling that he was seeing right through her, that maybe he could tell something was different about her. She held up her arms for him to pass Danny to her.

'I'll take you,' he said, bending to place the baby carefully on her lap. 'If Danny's sleeping we can leave him with Irene.'

'I'm not leaving Danny here alone,' she said stiffly, evading his eyes and staring out to sea.

'Why are you being like this? I thought things were going well between us. Last night—'

'All we did last night was make love—except it wasn't exactly making *love*,' she interrupted, her green eyes snapping back to his. 'We didn't have a proper conversation. Nothing meaningful happened between us.'

'Didn't making love mean anything to you?' he asked.

She stared at him in surprise, startled that he could dare to ask such a question considering the circumstances of their marriage.

'What would mean something to me is a little respect—a little freedom,' she said hotly. 'You've got me here against my wishes and I'm not even permitted to go shopping on my own.'

'What's so important about shopping?' He was keeping his voice level, but Carrie could hear undertones of suspicion hardening it. 'You can have anything you need delivered to the villa at any time you choose.'

'It's not about shopping,' she said, realising it had been a mistake to draw his attention so strongly to that. 'It's just that I don't want to be watched all the time,' she added, pointing up at the camera that was silently sweeping the beach. 'And I don't want to be locked up here all the time.'

'What do you want to buy that I can't see?' he pressed,

clearly not thrown off the scent by her attempted diversion. 'I thought we'd agreed to have no secrets between us.'

'No. *We* didn't agree that,' Carrie snapped. She was close to breaking point and she could feel tears pricking her eyes. She pressed her face instinctively against Danny's curls and closed her eyelids for a moment, drawing comfort from the feel of him in her arms. 'Like everything else in this marriage, *you* dictated it. *You* announced that was how it should be.'

Nik stood towering over her. She could feel his anger radiating out despite the rigid way he held himself. He leant down abruptly and took Danny from her, and before she had time to protest he pulled her to her feet and held her firmly in front of him.

'It's time to get back to the villa now.' He fixed her with eyes so cold that an involuntary shudder ran through her.

'Why?' she demanded, shaking his hand roughly off her arm and pulling Danny safely back into her embrace. 'Because *you* say so?'

'Because Danny's getting tired,' Nik said. 'And this conversation has gone as far as it's going to right now.'

Carrie stared at him for a second longer, suddenly feeling as if he'd wrong-footed her. Then she looked at Danny. Nik was right. He did look ready for his nap.

'You don't know he needs to sleep!' Carrie said crossly, irritated that despite their argument Nik had noticed the signs that Danny was getting tired before she did. 'You can't just sweep into his life and assume you know exactly what he needs.'

'We're going back.' Nik took her arm and set a brisk pace across the beach to the buggy.

'You go back if you're so determined to. I'm not going yet,' Carrie said. She fastened Danny securely in the pushchair with the harness, gripped the handles and moved him away from

Nik. 'I'll push him into the shade while he sleeps, and then I can enjoy the peace and quiet on my own.'

'You're not staying here alone,' Nik said through gritted teeth. 'Not when you're acting so erratically.'

'Why not? This bay is totally cut off. You don't seriously think I'll try to swim away?' Carrie turned towards the sea and made a sweeping gesture with her arm. Her eyes suddenly settled on a little boat that she hadn't noticed before. Without thinking she raised her arm and waved. 'Perhaps you're worried I'll flag down that boat!' she said.

'Don't be so ridiculous,' Nik grated, grabbing her arm and moving her roughly through the wrought-iron gateway. He followed closely with the buggy, pausing for a moment to bark something in rapid Greek into the intercom system just inside the gateway. Then, before Carrie had a chance to catch her breath, he was striding up the hill, pushing the buggy in front of him.

Her heart was pounding with shock and anger as she heard the heavy gate clang shut behind her. She turned and rattled it, then looked up at the camera, but nothing happened. She spun round and stared at Nik's retreating back.

She was trapped! Locked on his property once again.

And he was leaving with Danny! She started running up the hill immediately. He had a head start, and was already out of her sight, but she ran until her lungs were burning. She rounded the corner by the villa and saw Nik lifting Danny up.

'You're not going to take him away from me!' she cried. 'I'll never let you have him.'

'I was simply bringing him inside for his sleep,' he said. He let her take the baby but there was a lethal calmness in his eyes.

'You were trying to separate us,' she panted, still trying to catch her breath from the steep climb as she hugged Danny. 'Locking the gate and getting him away from me—'

'If I'd wanted to separate you from Danny I'd have locked you *off* my property, not *on* it,' he said witheringly, and he turned and walked away from her.

Nik pushed his chair back from his desk abruptly, stood up and strode across to his study window. The spectacular view across the mountains usually soothed him, made him thankful for this peaceful retreat away from his main residence in Athens. But that afternoon it didn't seem to be having its usual calming effect.

He turned and stalked across to the other window, looked out over the bay. The water glittered turquoise and the sky was still fine—which was more than could be said for his mood. Since they'd returned from the beach his mood had been growing darker and darker.

He thought about Carrie's behaviour that morning. She'd been happy and relaxed at first, but then everything had suddenly changed. It had seemed as if she was deliberately trying to pick a fight with him.

It was unacceptable. He wouldn't put up with that behaviour from anyone—and especially not from Carrie. She had agreed to this marriage and she understood his terms—or at least he'd thought she did.

'We need to talk.'

He turned to see Carrie standing in the doorway of his study. Her face was pale but resolute and her black hair was tied neatly at the nape of her neck. She was wearing the same flowery green dress she'd been wearing earlier. It was the dress she'd been wearing the first time they'd made love. The shade suited her, bringing out the colour of her eyes, and the soft draping fabric skimmed alluringly over her body, accentuating her curves.

'Yes, we do,' he agreed smoothly. Her silent arrival had

caught him slightly off guard, but he didn't allow it to show. 'Where's Danny?'

'Irene is playing with him,' she said. 'I don't want any distractions while we talk.'

'Good. Neither do I,' he said. She had calmed down, but he noticed an unusual brittleness underneath the surface of her composure. 'Come in and sit.'

'There's no need. I want to get on with this,' she said, not moving from her spot.

'I'm not having this discussion in a doorway.' Nik took her arm and pulled her into the room. 'Haven't you understood anything I've said to you about being my wife—about discretion?'

'Stop manhandling me!' Carrie wrenched her arm out of his grasp and glared at him. Her eyes were flashing green fire again and her calm composure was starting to crack.

'Then stop deliberately baiting me.' He closed his study door and looked at her meaningfully. 'When you married me you agreed to maintain the appearance of a normal happy marriage.'

'I wasn't baiting you!' Carrie gasped, rubbing her arm where his hand had held her. 'And there was no agreement between us! Like everything else, you *told* me what I had to do!'

'Well, listen carefully to what I'm telling you now,' Nik grated. 'You'll regret it if you try to pick a fight with me in public again. At the beach it was unacceptable—but arguing in front of my household is utterly unthinkable!'

'I wasn't trying to pick a fight,' she said, staring up at him towering over her. It was a large room, but Nik's presence seemed to fill it to capacity, making her shiver apprehensively. 'I was upset.'

Her heart was pounding and she was starting to question whether coming to talk to him now was the right decision. But no matter how much she balked at telling him her fears, in her heart she knew she had to take the initiative. By making the running it felt as if she was taking back some control of her life.

'What have you got to be upset about?' Nik asked, his derisive tone doing nothing to encourage her to tell him the truth. 'I told you—I'm not going to put up with petty squabbles and backbiting.'

She stared at his glowering face and swallowed, wondering how he was going to react. Despite the fact he was already bad-tempered, he couldn't be angry over possible pregnancy—he must know it was a potential outcome of their lovemaking. She might have forgotten about contraception, but surely he was far too experienced to have made the same mistake?

'Well?' he barked impatiently. 'Are you going to tell me what's bothering you?'

'I think I might be pregnant,' she blurted.

'What?' Nik stared at her in absolute shock. His chest felt rigid and drawing breath was suddenly hard.

'I…I realised at the beach this morning.' She stared up at him with wide eyes, looking uncertain even though she was the one who'd said the unfathomable thing.

'But you're on the pill,' Nik said. Blood was thudding relentlessly in his temples, making it almost impossible to think straight. 'If you forgot to take it you had a responsibility to tell me.'

'I didn't forget,' Carrie said. 'I'm not on the pill.'

'Then what are you playing at?' he demanded, raking his hands through his hair. 'Why did you tell me you were on the pill?'

'I didn't,' she insisted, shrinking back slightly.

'Did you plan to trap me in some way by getting pregnant with my child?' he growled. A horrible sensation churned in the pit of his stomach and he clenched his teeth, biting back the turmoil that was rising within him.

'Of course not!' Carrie snapped. 'I would *never* do something like that!'

'Then why the pretence?' Nik asked furiously. 'Why did you tell me in Menorca that you were protected?'

'I didn't!' Carrie gasped. Then clamped her hand over her mouth. A look of realisation flashed across her face as she suddenly recalled their conversation in the hotel room.

'You said we didn't have to worry about protection.' Nik stared at her. She looked pale and fragile, but at that moment all he felt was anger.

'I meant that it wasn't a problem because I never planned to sleep with you,' Carrie said, biting her lower lip and meeting his eyes with a cloudy green gaze. 'I'm sorry you misunderstood.'

'It's too late now. The damage is done,' Nik bit out, his voice uncompromisingly severe. 'Are you pregnant or not?'

'How would I know?' Carrie cried. 'It's not entirely my fault, you know! If you hadn't been so relentless this would never have happened.' She paused for breath, pushing her black fringe back from her eyes. 'I'm late—very late. But as I can't go shopping to buy a pregnancy test I can't say for certain.'

'You'll see the doctor this afternoon—as soon as possible,' Nik said, reaching into his pocket to pull out his mobile phone. It was unbearable not knowing.

'No!' Carrie's voice was firm, and she was standing with her hands on her hips in a determined posture. 'I'm not seeing a doctor—not yet. I want the freedom and privacy to find this out for myself.'

Nik put his phone down and looked at her through narrowed eyes.

'I want a home pregnancy test,' she said with conviction.

CHAPTER ELEVEN

AN UNEXPECTED numbness crept over Carrie as she watched the blue line appear on the test strip. But it only confirmed what she already knew in her heart. She was pregnant. She stood up stiffly to go to Nik. There was no reason to delay telling him the result.

She found him in his study. She paused at the open door, watching him standing by the large picture window. He hadn't seen her approach and was staring intently at the mountainous view.

Tension was evident in every line of his body, and in profile his face showed an expression that was as rigid as the rest of him.

Her heart started to patter, and she had the urge to back away, but at that exact moment he turned to look at her.

'Do you have the result?' His eyes were riveted on her and his voice was as hard as his body language

'Yes.' She walked into the study and closed the door. Soon the household would know, but for now she'd protect their privacy.

'Sit down,' he said, indicating two leather armchairs close to the window.

Carrie crossed the room and perched on the edge of one of the chairs. Nik sat down opposite. He drew his brows down so that his eyes were cast into shadow and his long fingers tightened on the arms of his leather chair.

She took a breath and, still holding his gaze, steeled herself to speak.

'It was positive.' She spoke clearly, but there was a slight tremor in her voice. 'I'm pregnant.'

She watched him, waiting for his response—but he said nothing.

A second later he stood up and walked out of the room.

Carrie stared after him in shock.

She'd expected him to be angry—she'd already seen that earlier—but she hadn't expected to glimpse the expression of pure horror that had flashed across his face as he left. He'd looked utterly appalled.

She stared at the empty doorway, feeling curiously detached from the situation. She was pregnant—her life was going to change for ever. And the man she was supposed to share it with had just walked out.

Carrie sat on a log in the shade, under a particularly large and ancient olive tree. The ground was covered with a layer of tiny white star-shaped flowers that had fallen from the gnarled branches, and Danny was picking them up and placing them in her outstretched hand.

It was a magical place for a child to play. The warm shade enclosed them and the lapping water just across the sweeping arc of pebbles glittered with the promise of even more fun still to be had. But Carrie wasn't enjoying herself as much as Danny.

She felt sick and tired, and slightly guilty because she'd gone off without telling Danny's new nanny where to find them, and now she couldn't summon up the will to trek back up the path to the villa.

It wasn't finding the energy for the climb—although she

was tired, she was still fit—it was the awful feeling of claustrophobia that swamped her in the villa. She had no freedom, and it felt as if she was being watched all the time.

She hadn't wanted a nanny, but Nik had been immovable on the subject.

'I've hired someone to help with Danny,' he'd said one afternoon, about a week after the confirmation of her pregnancy. 'You need to take better care of yourself.'

'I'm fine,' Carrie replied, feeling resentful that this was the first time he'd come anywhere near her or Danny for days. He hadn't asked how they were—or spoken directly about her pregnancy. 'I don't need any help.'

'A nanny will give you time to rest,' Nik said.

'I'm not giving Danny up for someone else to care for.' She stared at him crossly, suddenly determined to get him to acknowledge the child she was carrying. 'And you know that when this baby is born I will look after it myself.'

'You need to be responsible,' Nik said. 'And that means accepting some help.'

'I don't need any help,' Carrie said stubbornly, irritated that he still hadn't shown any sign that he accepted their unborn child. 'Other parents manage on their own.'

'*You* don't need to,' Nik said categorically. 'I won't allow you to run yourself into the ground. You should rest now—you look tired.'

'Don't patronise me!' Carrie snapped. 'I'm pregnant—not ill.'

'Nevertheless, you need to rest,' Nik said, turning on his heel and striding away.

And that, Carrie reflected, had been the closest he'd come to acknowledging her pregnancy.

She laid her hand on her still flat stomach and looked out at the peacock-blue sea. She liked this shady olive grove next to the beach; it was the only place she felt at ease, and over the last month she had spent more and more time here. Danny liked it too, and would spend hours happily sorting the silver-grey pebbles or playing by the water.

A movement caught her eye and she saw the nanny, Helen, walking along the beach away from them. She must have come through the gate and turned in the opposite direction.

'I'm over here, Helen!' Carrie called, and waved, hoping to catch her attention. She was a nice Greek girl who spoke perfect English, and despite Carrie's resistance to having a nanny she'd found that she liked her. She didn't want her to needlessly walk all the way to the other end of the bay and back.

'Hello, there!' Helen called, ducking under a low olive branch and grinning at Danny. 'What have you got there?'

He squealed with delight and deposited a handful of crushed olive blossom onto her outstretched palm.

'Sorry you had to search for me,' Carrie said. 'I didn't seem to have the energy to climb the hill.'

'That's all right.' Helen smiled brightly, and Carrie suddenly had the strangest feeling that maybe she was also happy to get away from the villa for an afternoon. Being around Nik was anything but relaxing, and he'd got into the routine of coming to play with Danny during Carrie's after-noon break.

It hadn't occurred to her before, but Nik's presence must be totally overpowering for a young girl—especially consid-ering the black mood he'd been in since the discovery of Carrie's pregnancy.

'May I take him down to the water's edge?' Helen asked.

'Of course,' Carrie replied, putting his hat firmly on his head. 'He loves to splash, and he's already covered with sunblock.'

She watched Helen take Danny down to the lapping waves and sighed. Sometimes it was hard to believe how different her life had become from her life spent in London, doing two jobs just to make ends meet. Despite the hard work, she'd been happy then. Now she wasn't so sure.

In her mind there was no doubt that Danny was enjoying being here. But she couldn't help thinking about herself and the child she was carrying. Was this the right place for *them*?

Nik seemed to be actively avoiding her. He hadn't spent any time with her during the day and he never came to her at night. Was this how her life was going to be? Totally isolated, with a husband who didn't want to know her, didn't want to know the child she was carrying?

A movement caught her eye and she glanced up to see Nik. He was standing in the sunshine just below her, on the edge of the beach.

He looked amazing. His dark hair gleamed in the sunlight and his bronze skin glowed with vitality, but her gaze slid straight to the expression on his face.

He hadn't spotted her under the trees. All his attention was focussed on Danny. An incredible smile spread across his handsome features and she felt her heart skip a beat.

If only he would look at *her* like that.

She sucked in a startled breath and frowned as she looked at Nik. Why should she care how he looked at her?

Because being ignored by him hurt her feelings. No, it was worse than that. She kept remembering the horrified expression he'd had when she'd told him she was pregnant. He hadn't been able to get out of the room quickly enough, but she'd still seen his face. That horrified look still haunted her.

He'd started playing with Danny now, and Helen stood awkwardly to one side. As Carrie watched them heading along the water's edge together, splashing as they went, she felt a cloud of misery settle over her.

Now Nik was on the beach there was nothing else to look at. Whenever he was around she found her gaze drawn to him like a bee to a honey pot. She noticed his hair had been trimmed, and his skin was a shade darker. His bronze skin obviously tanned easily in the Greek sun, despite the number of hours he spent inside on the telephone or his computer.

She wondered who had cut his hair. She'd been away from home so long that her own fringe was in desperate need of a trim. She bit her lip and frowned—*this* was her home now, and she needed to start thinking of it that way.

She drew her knees up to her chest and wondered why she felt so unhappy. Nik had come down to the beach to see Danny, and that was good. But that was just it—he obviously couldn't stand to see *her*. He always came to see Danny when he was with Helen, because he simply couldn't bear to spend any time with her.

Suddenly her vision blurred with tears. Her eyes filled up as she watched Nik playing with Danny and no one knew or cared. She hugged her knees tightly, suddenly overtaken by sadness. Why did she long for Nik to come under the olive tree and talk to her?

She remembered how happy she'd felt the night he'd come back from his business trip. He'd made love to her and it had been truly wonderful. The following morning she'd been filled with happiness and everything had felt perfect. But that had been just a hollow illusion that had quickly fallen apart.

She gazed at Nik through a haze of tears, wishing she could have that feeling back. For such a short time she had been full of happiness, full of love.

She sucked in a startled breath and stared at Nik with wide, shocked eyes.

She loved him.

Somehow she had fallen in love with Nik.

Her heart started to thump in her chest and her mouth

suddenly felt dry. It couldn't be true. She couldn't have fallen in love without realising it.

She pressed her front teeth into her lower lip to stop her jaw trembling. How was it possible? Did she really love him or was she just imagining it? She pushed shaking fingers through her hair, brushing her long fringe back from her eyes, and looking at Nik.

It was true. She loved him.

She could feel her love for him flowing though her, making her chest ache, causing a tremor to run through her from the tips of her fingers to the ends of her toes.

But wasn't being in love supposed to be a good thing? If she was in love with Nik, why did watching him make her feel so bad?

She knew the answer.

Because he didn't love her.

CHAPTER TWELVE

BY THE time Danny was bathed and ready for bed that night Carrie felt utterly drained. It had been a difficult day—and realising that she'd fallen in love with Nik had made everything seem so much harder.

She sat on the rug with Danny before bed, and an overwhelming feeling of loneliness welled up inside her. The time she spent alone with Danny had always been precious to her, but now it was all she had.

She felt like a traitor—to herself, to Danny, and also to her unborn child. She was locked in a marriage with a man who would never love her. Surely they all deserved more than that?

Without her compliance none of this could have happened—yet what choice had she had? There was no doubt that Nik would have kept his word to take Danny away from her if she hadn't married him. And now her innocent unborn child would be part of this appalling charade as well.

Suddenly an impatient cry cut through her thoughts. It was Danny.

She lifted her head to see him standing on the other side of the room, waving a large toy at her.

'Sorry, Danny,' she said. 'Was I ignoring you?'

With her attention now firmly fixed on him, Danny

squealed with delight and threw the toy down. Then, with a totally mischievous look on his cute little face, he took a step towards her. Then another. Then one more.

'You're walking!' Carrie breathed, her worries momentarily blotted out as a smile of wonder spread over her face. She held out her arms towards him. 'Come on,' she called in encouragement. 'You can do it!'

Danny squealed again and took three more steps towards her, before losing his balance and veering off to one side.

'You can walk!' She swung him up into her arms and hugged him tightly. 'Clever, clever boy!'

She beamed at him and ruffled his hair. His button eyes were shining and he looked as proud of his achievement as she was.

She sank down onto the cream sofa and smiled at him. It was incredible—Danny was walking. It was one of those all-important milestones. She should go and tell Nik —he would be so proud, too.

She stopped and bit her lip.

She couldn't go to Nik. He'd made it crystal-clear that he didn't want to see her. He might be interested in Danny's achievement, but she wasn't to be the one to tell him. Now he asked Helen how Danny was getting on. She would pass on the information tomorrow.

Suddenly tears welled up in her eyes. She wanted someone to share her joy over Danny's milestone. And she wanted someone to share her unborn baby's milestones.

Tomorrow she was going to the hospital for her first scan. Nik knew about it—he'd seen the appointment letter—but he'd never even bothered to mention it to her. He simply didn't care.

Carrie felt cold inside. Cold and numb.

She lay down on the sofa, hoping for sleep to block out her misery, but the sleep she craved would not come. The leather was cool and ungiving beneath the skin of her cheek and it seemed to draw out the heat of her body through the thin cotton of her dress. She hugged a cushion, but it provided no warmth or comfort.

She couldn't believe things had come to this. She'd just wanted to do what was best for Danny, to make sure his future was secure, but as she looked into her own future all she could see was darkness. She felt as if she was being sucked into a black hole and the life was being slowly crushed out of her.

Nik stood on the balcony and stared out to sea. There wasn't another human being in sight, which was normally how he liked it when he had the opportunity to take a break from work. But today it seemed curiously empty.

He'd grown used to having Carrie and Danny around the villa, and even though he'd kept his distance he liked to have some idea where they were.

He started back towards his study, but then heard Danny's happy cries coming from the garden at the front of the villa. He looked out of a window and saw him playing with his nanny. He frowned and headed out to the garden.

'Why do you have Danny now?' Nik called, walking quickly towards them. 'This is not the time of day you normally spend with him.'

'Mrs Kristallis has gone to the hospital,' Helen said. 'Her appointment letter said that they prefer you not to take children with you when you go for your scan.'

Nik stopped and stared at Helen.

'The scan is this morning?'

'Yes,' Helen said. 'I thought you knew.'

Without another word Nik turned and strode away across the lawn.

* * *

The radiographer rolled a hand-held probe across the gel on Carrie's stomach and strange echoey noises started coming from the ultrasound machine. Carrie stared at the monitor, trying to see her baby, but she didn't understand the shifting black and white images that flashed before her.

Where was her baby? Was it supposed to take this long to get a picture of her baby on the screen?

'Is everything all right?' she asked.

The radiographer didn't reply, and Carrie belatedly remembered what she'd discovered earlier—she didn't speak English. Instead she kept frowning at the monitor with a look of intense concentration on her face and continued to move the probe across Carrie's stomach.

She lay still as stone, trying to keep calm, but horrible fears were building inside her. She tried to make her mind go blank, to relax, but it was impossible. How long was it supposed to take to see her baby on the screen? She knew it had only been moments, but it seemed like an age.

She wished she wasn't alone. She wished the radiographer spoke English.

She wished she knew her baby was all right.

Suddenly the door opened and Nik came into the room. He took one startled look at her face, then was by her side in two powerful strides.

'What's wrong?' he asked, taking her shaking hand in his.

'I don't know. Nothing, maybe.' Carrie's voice trembled as she spoke and she felt tears prick in her eyes. 'She doesn't speak English, and I haven't seen my baby on the screen yet.'

Nik swore in Greek, then spoke rapidly to the radiographer.

'It sometimes takes a moment to get the probe in the right position.' Nik translated what the radiographer said to him. His voice was comforting and he squeezed her hand reassuringly, but Carrie saw from his body language that he was tense.

At that moment the whomp, whomp, whomp of a heart-beat filled the room.

'Look—there's the baby, and there's the heart beating.' The relief in Nik's voice reverberated through her, but she had to see for herself.

She stared at the screen with wide eyes, desperately trying to make out the shape of the baby, then suddenly she saw its tiny beating heart, pulsing like a little beacon on the fuzzy black and white screen.

Her lip quivered and she squeezed her eyes shut to stop the tears of relief from falling. For a moment she'd been really scared that something was wrong.

'The radiographer has to make some measurements,' Nik said, holding her hand in both of his.

He looked at the screen, watching the little body come in and out of focus as the radiographer moved the probe about, trying to get the best angle for her measurements.

Suddenly it struck him like a thunderbolt out of the blue—he was looking at his baby!

His heart thudded powerfully in his chest.

He was going to be a father. It was the first time that fact had really sunk in. When Carrie had told him she was pregnant he'd been so shocked he hadn't known what to do. He'd understood it in his mind—although he'd shied away from thinking about it—but now he felt it in his heart. That little figure wriggling on the screen was his baby, and he already loved him.

'Look—I can see its head,' Carrie breathed. 'And its little arms and legs.'

'It's incredible,' Nik agreed, studying his baby intently. 'Look—he's really moving, and kicking his legs about. Can you feel that?'

'No,' Carrie paused and looked down at her still flat stomach. 'You don't feel them moving till later. And we don't know what sex it is yet.'

Nik watched her as she turned her attention back to the monitor. The moment he'd come into the room and seen her stark white face and frightened green eyes he'd been racked with guilt. She shouldn't have come to the scan alone—he should have been with her. It was his responsibility.

But now his feelings ran deeper than guilt and responsibility. Suddenly he was feeling an unprecedented wave of protectiveness towards her. Despite the tremulous smile on her face she looked so vulnerable that it made his chest ache. She was even paler than before, if that was possible, and there were dark circles under her eyes.

'I'm sorry,' Nik said. 'I should have been here with you from the start.'

'I thought you weren't interested in coming.' The haunted look in her eyes as she turned to meet his gaze sent a shudder running through him. 'You never even mentioned the scan, even though I know you knew about my appointment.'

'I didn't intend for you to come alone,' Nik said, breaking eye contact and looking back at the screen. 'I just didn't realise it was so soon.'

Carrie looked at Nik. He was staring at the baby on the screen with a look of awe on his face. She was used to seeing intense expressions on his face—he was a man who felt things passionately and didn't mind her knowing the strength of his feelings—but his expression of open wonder as he gazed at the image of the baby—*their* baby—was strangely affecting.

A mixture of emotions stirred inside her. He did care about the baby. He might not care enough about her to remember the scan appointment—but he *did* care about the baby.

He was still holding her hand, and for a moment his grip

was strong and warm. If he cared about the baby she had something to hang on to—something to give her strength.

She looked at the screen but the image was gone, and suddenly she realised that the radiographer had put the probe down. She wanted to catch one last look at her baby, but the radiographer was speaking to Nik, holding out a small printed photo.

'Everything is fine.' He handed the photo of their baby to her. 'You'll need another scan later on, but for now everything looks good.'

Carrie stared at the little black and white photo. It was her baby. It was real.

'We can go when you're ready,' Nik said, taking the wad of tissue the radiographer was holding out and gently smoothing it over Carrie's stomach, wiping off the lubricating gel that had been used for the scan.

Carrie lay still, surprised by the tenderness of his actions. He'd touched her before, but his touches had always been loaded with sensuality. Now he was smoothing the tissue softly over her skin in a tender, caring way.

A frisson of disappointment surprised her. Did that mean that now she was to be the mother of his child she no longer interested him on a sexual level? She wasn't feeling very sexy—she was tired and nauseous most of the time—but the idea that Nik no longer thought of her in that way was horribly upsetting.

'I'll drive you home,' Nik said, gently pulling her blouse down into position and sliding his arm behind her shoulders to help her up into a sitting position. 'Unless there is anywhere else you'd like to go now we're out?'

'Home is fine,' Carrie said.

Nik's arm was still around her shoulders and she leant against his strong chest, letting the heat of his body warm her.

The scan photo was in her hand, and as she looked at the image of her baby she felt Nik's arm tighten protectively round her. For a moment she let herself imagine that they were a normal loving couple, sharing in the experience of seeing their baby for the first time.

It had been awesome to see the baby, and she knew Nik had been affected by it, too. It was amazing to think there was a baby growing inside her

But for Carrie it was overshadowed by stress and sadness. She loved Nik so much that being close to him, knowing he didn't return her feelings, was like a physical pain. Leaning into his embrace was a bittersweet mixture of joy and regret.

'Let's go to the car if you're ready?' Nik said.

'All right.' She stood up, and they walked outside to the car park together.

'You sit down and rest a moment,' Nik said, opening the door of an open-topped black sports car that Carrie had never seen before. 'I'll tell Spiro to head back on his own.'

Carrie slid into the passenger seat of Nik's car, feeling more alone than ever. She missed the comfort of his arm around her shoulder, and suddenly she hated the fact that she'd never even seen his car before. She'd only ever been in the limousine with Spiro, and it had never occurred to her that Nik had a personal car that he drove on his own.

This morning was the first time Nik had spent more than a couple of minutes with her since she'd told him she was pregnant, and she had realised two things.

She loved Nik, and she craved his company even more than she'd thought.

Being with him, especially with him acting as if he cared about her and her unborn child, was a kind of torture. A succession of emotions churned through her, knotting painfully inside her chest and tightening her throat so that she could hardly breathe. Tears welled up in her eyes and there was nothing she could do to stop them falling.

Nik walked back towards his convertible, thinking how lucky he'd been not to have missed the scan altogether. Seeing his baby on the screen had been simply amazing—but because of his reluctance to accept how fast his life was changing he'd almost been too late. He wouldn't let anything like that happen again.

Suddenly he caught sight of Carrie's face in the rearview mirror of his car. What he saw stopped him in his tracks.

She was staring at the ultrasound picture with tears rolling silently down her cheeks. She shivered slightly while she wept, but it wasn't her tears that wrenched his heart so cruelly—it was the look of utter desolation on her face.

Almost without realising it, he started walking towards her. She turned her head slightly as he approached, and he caught a glimpse of her tear-stained face, but then she wiped her hands quickly over her cheeks and pulled her sunglasses down from on top of her head to hide her red eyes. Her hand was shaking and there was a fragility about her that tore at him painfully.

It hurt that she didn't want him to know how she was feeling—but he knew it was his fault. He had driven a wedge between them, and now they were so far apart emotionally that she couldn't bear him to see her upset.

But he had to find out what was wrong. She was holding the scan picture. It had never occurred to him to wonder whether she was happy to be pregnant.

He opened the passenger door and knelt beside the low-slung car, taking her hand in his.

'I'm sorry,' he said. 'I'm so sorry I wasn't here for you.'

'It's all right.' Carrie's voice was quiet, but steady. If he hadn't seen the tears for himself he would never have guessed that he'd caught her crying. 'I'm glad you managed to come when you did.'

'You gave me a shock when you told me you were pregnant,' Nik said. 'I'm sorry I reacted the way I did, but I realised today how happy I am to be having a child.'

Carrie didn't speak. She looked small and wretched—a million miles away from the fiery woman she'd been when they first met. And it was *his* doing.

The muscle of his heart clenched and his throat tightened painfully. He couldn't be responsible for making Carrie so miserable.

But he'd married her for a good reason. This was all about doing what was right for his brother's son. And now for his own unborn child.

Or was it?

Realisation hit him like a blow. It was about Carrie. Ever since the day they'd met, it had always been about Carrie.

Of course he'd wanted her, from the moment he laid eyes on her in that skimpy red dress. She'd been pure sex on legs—enough to make any man's libido shoot into overdrive. But each time he'd seen her after that the need to possess her had deepened, and now he knew it wasn't just sexual.

She was an extraordinary person. She did and felt everything with such passion. Her inherent vitality had drawn him to her from the start, and beneath her sparkling personality he'd been aware of the depths of love and devotion she felt for Danny. She had given up a lot to look after him, and even though it was a challenge, both financially and practically, she had thrown herself into it with the energy that characterised everything she did.

The more he thought about it, the more he realised that every decision he'd made, every action he'd taken, had been about Carrie, about how to make sure she became part of his life.

And now he had won her. She was his wife. She was having his baby.

Why did her unhappiness cut him so cruelly?

Because he loved her!

His heart hammered in his chest and he felt the prickle of sweat break out on his brow. He had fallen in love with Carrie.

He stared at her beautiful face in shock, hardly able to comprehend what he'd just realised—then suddenly he saw a teardrop trickle out from under her dark glasses.

'Oh, my love,' he cried, lifting her sunglasses gently away and cupping her face so that he could make eye contact. 'Please don't cry.'

Carrie stared at him in bewilderment. Tears blurred her vision, but Nik's expression seemed to reflect the agony she felt.

'I'm sorry,' she gulped. 'I didn't mean to… I can't…'

'I'm the one who's sorry,' Nik said. 'I've done this to you. I've made you so unhappy.'

Suddenly he leant forward and started showering her face with gentle kisses. His hands slid down to her shoulders and he knelt before her, supporting her tenderly with his strong arms.

Carrie closed her eyes and gave herself over to the feelings his kisses evoked. One last time she would allow herself to believe it meant something to him. One last time she would blot out the world and just be there with Nik, her lover.

'I can't bear that I've caused you so much pain,' he burst out. 'I love you!'

'What?' Carrie gasped. Surely she couldn't have heard correctly.

'Please forgive me for putting you through so much.' He held her away from him so that he could fix her in his intense gaze.

'What did you say?' Carrie asked, her voice hardly more than a whisper.

'I'm sorry for hurting you,' he said. 'And I'm sorry you're having a baby before you're ready for it.'

'Before that,' she said. Her heart was racing, but she couldn't let herself believe she'd heard correctly.

'I love you,' Nik said.

Carrie stared at him in bewilderment. A glimmer of hope was growing in her heart, but she wouldn't give free rein to it—not yet. Nik had said he loved her—which was unimaginably wonderful—but for some reason he seemed upset about it.

'I have fallen in love with you,' Nik said simply 'And I can't bear that I've caused you so much misery.'

Carrie finally let the happiness swell inside her.

She smiled with wonder as things fell into place at last, and she lifted her hands to cup his face tenderly.

'You were so sad.' Nik's expression was still troubled. 'It was marrying me and getting pregnant that made you miserable.'

'I was sad because I love *you* so much and I thought you'd never love me,' Carrie said tentatively 'I was always happy to be having your baby. I just wished our marriage was real.'

'You love *me*?' Nik asked, a look of almost incredulous joy slowly lighting his face.

She nodded and smiled up at him tremulously, her happiness overflowing as at last they understood each other.

Nik gave a shout of pure joy and seized her in a rough embrace, bounding to his feet with an exuberance that lifted her clean out of the car. Once again her eyes were misty, but this time they were tears of happiness, and she didn't try to hide them. He kissed her fiercely, then swung her round and round before setting her down, still encircled by his arms.

She laughed, thinking she had never seen him look more handsome. He was incredible. The love he felt was written all over his face, animating his features and lighting him from within. At that instant she knew it was real. He loved her as much as she loved him.

She gazed up at him, basking in his adoration, never wanting him to release her.

'You are so amazing!' Nik seized her and almost crushed her in his enthusiasm.

'So are you,' Carrie gasped, thinking how true that was, from the very bottom of her heart.

'You've given me my life,' he said suddenly. 'Before I met you my life was hollow. I was hollow.'

'That's how I felt last night,' Carrie admitted quietly. 'And during the scan. I love you so much that I could hardly bear to be with you, knowing that you didn't return my feelings—but I couldn't even stand to think about life without you.'

'We'll never be apart.' Nik's voice was suddenly gruff as he pulled her down into the sports car with him. 'You and Danny are everything to me and we will always be together.'

Carrie sank down against the comfort of Nik's steady heartbeat, revelling in the strength of his arms embracing her. For the first time in her life she felt as if she'd finally come home.

'The three of us will always be together,' she repeated, smiling dreamily up into the face of the man she loved. 'Well, the four of us,' she added, resting her hand gently on her stomach.

Nik looked down at her, an incredible feeling of love and pride spreading through him.

'Maybe we'll spend a few moments on our own,' he answered, a mischievous twinkle in his eyes. 'Just the two of us.'

* * * * *

THE ROYAL HOUSE OF NIROLI
Always passionate, always proud

The richest royal family in the world—
united by blood and passion,
torn apart by deceit and desire

Nestled in the azure blue of the Mediterranean Sea, the majestic island of Niroli has prospered for centuries. The Ficrezza men have worn the crown with passion and pride since ancient times. But now, as the king's health declines, and his two sons have been tragically killed, the crown is in jeopardy.

The clock is ticking—a new heir must be found before the king is forced to abdicate. By royal decree the internationally scattered members of the Fierezza family are summoned to claim their destiny. But any person who takes the throne must do so according to The Rules of the Royal House of Niroli. Soon secrets and rivalries emerge as the descendents of this ancient royal line vie for position and power. Only a true Fierezza can become ruler—a person dedicated to their country, their people…and their eternal love!

Each month starting in July 2007,
Harlequin Presents is delighted to bring you
an exciting installment from
THE ROYAL HOUSE OF NIROLI,
in which you can follow the epic search
for the true Nirolian king.
Eight heirs, eight romances, eight fantastic stories!

Here's your chance to enjoy a sneak preview of the first book delivered to you by royal decree…

FIVE minutes later she was standing immobile in front of the study's window, her original purpose of coming in forgotten, as she stared in shocked horror at the envelope she was holding. Waves of heat followed by icy chill surged through her body. She could hardly see the address now through her blurred vision, but the crest on its left-hand front corner stood out, its *royal* crest, followed by the address: *HRH Prince Marco of Niroli…*

She didn't hear Marco's key in the apartment door, she didn't even hear him calling out her name. Her shock was so great that nothing could penetrate it. It encased her in a kind of bubble, which only concentrated the torment of what she was suffering and branded it on her brain so that it could never be forgotten. It was only finally pierced by the sudden opening of the study door as Marco walked in.

"Welcome home, *Your Highness*. I suppose I ought to curtsy." She waited, praying that he would laugh and tell her that she had got it all wrong, that the envelope she was holding, addressing him as Prince Marco of Niroli, was some silly mistake. But like a tiny candle flame shivering vulnerably in the dark, her hope trembled fearfully. And then the look in Marco's eyes extinguished it as cruelly as a hand placed callously over a dying person's face to stem their last breath.

"Give that to me," he demanded, taking the envelope from her.

"It's too late, Marco," Emily told him brokenly. "I know the truth now…." She dug her teeth in her lower lip to try to force back her own pain.

"You had no right to go through my desk," Marco shot back at her furiously, full of loathing at being caught off-guard and forced into a position in which he was in the wrong, making him determined to find something he could accuse Emily of. "I trusted you…."

Emily could hardly believe what she was hearing. "No, you didn't trust me, Marco, and you didn't trust me because you knew that I couldn't trust you. And you knew that because you're a liar, and liars don't trust people because they know that they themselves cannot be trusted." She not only felt sick, she also felt as though she could hardly breathe. "You are Prince Marco of Niroli…. How could you not tell me who you are and still live with me as intimately as we have lived together?" she demanded brokenly.

"Stop being so ridiculously dramatic," Marco demanded fiercely. "You are making too much of the situation."

"Too much?" Emily almost screamed the words at him. "When were you going to tell me, Marco? Perhaps you just planned to walk away without telling me anything? After all, what do my feelings matter to you?"

"Of course they matter." Marco stopped her sharply. "And it was in part to protect them, and you, that I decided not to inform you when my grandfather first announced that he intended to step down from the throne and hand it on to me."

"To protect me?" Emily nearly choked on her fury. "Hand on the throne? No wonder you told me when you first took me to bed that all you wanted was sex. You *knew* that was the only kind of relationship there could ever be between us! You *knew* that one day you would be Niroli's king. No doubt you are expected to marry a princess. Is she picked out for you already, your *royal* bride?"

* * * * *

Look for THE FUTURE KING'S PREGNANT MISTRESS
by Penny Jordan in July 2007,
from Harlequin Presents,
available wherever books are sold.

**Two billionaires, one Greek, one Spanish—
will they claim their unwilling brides?**

Meet Sandor and Miguel, men who've taken all the prizes
when it comes to looks, power, wealth and arrogance.
Now they want marriage with two beautiful women.
But this time, for the first time, both Mediterranean
billionaires have met their matches and it will take more
than money or cool to tame their unwilling mistresses!

Miguel made Amber Taylor feel beautiful for the
first time. For Miguel it was supposed to be a
two-week affair…but now he'd taken the most
precious gift of all—her innocence!

TAKEN:
THE SPANIARD'S VIRGIN
Miguel's story (#2644)

by Lucy Monroe

On sale July 2007.

www.eHarlequin.com

REQUEST YOUR FREE BOOKS!

HARLEQUIN *Presents*

2 FREE NOVELS PLUS 2 FREE GIFTS!

PASSION GUARANTEED SEDUCTION

YES! Please send me 2 FREE Harlequin Presents® novels and my 2 FREE gifts. After receiving them, if I don't wish to receive any more books, I can return the shipping statement marked "cancel." If I don't cancel, I will receive 6 brand-new novels every month and be billed just $3.80 per book in the U.S., or $4.47 per book in Canada, plus 25¢ shipping and handling per book and applicable taxes, if any*. That's a savings of close to 15% off the cover price! I understand that accepting the 2 free books and gifts places me under no obligation to buy anything. I can always return a shipment and cancel at any time. Even if I never buy another book from Harlequin, the two free books and gifts are mine to keep forever.

106 HDN FEXK   306 HDN EEXV

Name	(PLEASE PRINT)	
Address		Apt. #
City	State/Prov.	Zip/Postal Code

Signature (if under 18, a parent or guardian must sign)

Mail to the **Harlequin Reader Service®**:
IN U.S.A.: P.O. Box 1867, Buffalo, NY 14240-1867
IN CANADA: P.O. Box 609, Fort Erie, Ontario L2A 5X3

Not valid to current Harlequin Presents subscribers.

Want to try two free books from another line?
Call 1-800-873-8635 or visit www.morefreebooks.com.

* Terms and prices subject to change without notice. NY residents add applicable sales tax. Canadian residents will be charged applicable provincial taxes and GST. This offer is limited to one order per household. All orders subject to approval. Credit or debit balances in a customer's account(s) may be offset by any other outstanding balance owed by or to the customer. Please allow 4 to 6 weeks for delivery.

Your Privacy: Harlequin is committed to protecting your privacy. Our Privacy Policy is available online at www.eHarlequin.com or upon request from the Reader Service. From time to time we make our lists of customers available to reputable firms who may have a product or service of interest to you. If you would prefer we not share your name and address, please check here. ☐

HP07